SILVER
RAIN

LOIS PETERSON

ORCA BOOK PUBLISHERS

Library and Archives Canada Cataloguing in Publication

Peterson, Lois J., 1952-
Silver rain / written by Lois Peterson.

ISBN 978-1-55469-280-4

I. Title.
PS8631.E832S59 2010   jC813'.6   C2010-903575-5

First published in the United States, 2010
Library of Congress Control Number: 2010929089

Summary: Elsie's father has disappeared and, as the Depression wears on, the family becomes desperate for money. But is a dance marathon any way to solve a family's problems?

10% of author royalties from this book helps support the South Fraser Women's Services Society in Surrey, BC.

Mixed Sources
Product group from well-managed forests,
controlled sources and recycled wood or fiber
www.fsc.org Cert no. SW-COC-000952
© 1996 Forest Stewardship Council

Orca Book Publishers is dedicated to preserving the environment and has printed this book on paper certified by the Forest Stewardship Council.

Orca Book Publishers gratefully acknowledges the support for its publishing programs provided by the following agencies: the Government of Canada through the Canada Book Fund and the Canada Council for the Arts, and the Province of British Columbia through the BC Arts Council and the Book Publishing Tax Credit.

Cover Design by Teresa Bubela
Cover photo by Getty Images
Typesetting by Jasmine Devonshire
Author photo by E. Henry

ORCA BOOK PUBLISHERS
PO Box 5626, STN. B
VICTORIA, BC CANADA
V8R 6S4

ORCA BOOK PUBLISHERS
PO Box 468
CUSTER, WA USA
98240-0468

www.orcabook.com
Printed and bound in Canada.

13 12 11 10 • 4 3 2 1

For my dear friend, Elsie Ramberg, who "lent" me her name, although this is not her story.

CHAPTER ONE

When Elsie slammed the mailbox shut, it shuddered on its post.

She opened the lid again and peered inside one more time. But no matter how many times she looked, there was still no letter from Father.

She stood under the drooping lilac tree with her hands shoved in her overall pockets, staring at the front door of the house a few feet away. Even though her family hadn't lived in the house for more than a year, she still thought of it as *her* front door. With *her* yellow tulip in the stained-glass panel she'd helped Father install.

And it was still her mailbox too. Even if she did have to share it with Jimmy Tipson's family.

Elsie kicked the wooden post, pulled her hat down tighter over her bangs and tipped her head back to watch the rain. It was thin and shimmery, like the silverfish that swam out of the cupboards in the garage that was now her home. Maybe the rain would help the crops grow again. Mother said if there was more wheat, there would be more jobs, and people could feed their families and stay in their own homes. It didn't make much sense to Elsie, even though her grade-five teacher had explained about the Depression more than once. How long would it take for things to get back to normal? Whatever that was.

She was about to turn away when a voice called, "Hey. You. Get away from here!" Jimmy stood on the porch, his fists on his hips. "You're trespassing, you know." Although he was in Elsie's class, he'd never had anything to do with her until his parents bought her family's house from the bank. Now he was always on the lookout, poking fun at her, blocking her way on the sidewalk.

Elsie pulled off her hat and slapped it against her leg. "I can stand here if I want. It's *my* mailbox too, you know."

"Who's going to write *you*?" jeered Jimmy.

"None of your business," Elsie yelled.

"Maybe I have your letter. Ever think of that?" As Jimmy opened his mouth to say more, the stone Elsie threw caught him on the lip. "Hey!"

"Hey, yourself." Elsie picked up another stone.

This one landed at Jimmy's feet. "Stop that," he screeched, "or I'll come down there and belt you one."

"Just try it." She held a stone in the air. "Ready for this, then? You big bully."

"Okay. Okay." He dabbed his lip with his fingers and looked at them. "I'm bleeding."

"You're just a big baby."

Jimmy's chin trembled as he pulled a handkerchief from his pocket.

"Want me to call your mother?" Elsie asked. "If you like, I can walk right up those steps. I'll fetch your mother so she can kiss you better."

"Just leave me alone." Jimmy stuffed his handkerchief back in his pocket. "Look in the mailbox all you want. See if I care."

"I will," said Elsie. "See if I don't." She tossed another stone in the air and caught it. "I'll keep checking this mailbox until I get the letter I'm waiting for. And nothing you can do will stop me."

She waited until Jimmy had gone back inside, slamming the door behind him, before she dropped the stone. Then Elsie pulled up the collar of her old brown corduroy jacket and, without looking back, ducked under the tree and ran through the rain to the shabby garage at the end of the yard.

"There you are, then," said her grandmother as Elsie ran indoors. Nan was pinning damp washing to the lines strung across the room. "I could have done with your help." She snapped a tea towel straight and pegged it up.

Sometimes Elsie thought her home looked like a spider's web, with the wash lines zigzagging across it. A curtain separating the living room from the bedroom hung from another line. Yet another curtain created a place for Uncle Dannell's cot—where Dog Bob sometimes slept too—and a separate nook for the big bed that Elsie shared with Nan and Mother.

A striped blanket hung from a rod above the front door to keep out the drafts.

Elsie slumped into the armchair that sat between the old kitchen table and a tile-topped cabinet. Father's armchair. Two battered wooden chairs and a short bench pushed under the table took up so much of the room that there was hardly space for them all: Nan, Mother, Uncle Dannell, Elsie and Dog Bob.

Father used to sit in this chair after he got home from the jewelry store each night. "Mrs. Cohen came for a brooch for her new jacket," he might tell Elsie.

Or, "Your Miss Beastly—oops—Miss Beeston? She wanted a match for a pearl earring she lost. Should have been home giving you an A for your English composition, I suggested."

But the shop was gone now. And Father too. Elsie shoved her fists into her eyes to stop the tears.

"Ernest came looking for you," said Nan as she pegged one last towel over Elsie's head. "Something important, he said. He plumb wears me out." Her voice was muffled behind the laundry.

Elsie jumped up. "I'll go over."

"You'll do no such thing, miss. I said he should come back after supper," Nan told her.

Elsie picked at a splinter on the table. Then she said, "Ernest is going to be a newspaperman. Did you know? He collects the news so he can write about it."

"He'll go far, I don't think." Some of Nan's strange expressions made sense, some didn't. Elsie smiled as she took the laundry basket her grandmother handed her. "What are you laughing about?" Nan asked. "Go hang this back on the wall next to Dannell's bed."

"Where's Mother?" asked Elsie when she came back.

"Mrs. Tipson gave Peg an afternoon's work," said Nan. "Now, take that hat off in the house. How many times."

Elsie hoped Mother hadn't seen her throwing stones at Jimmy. She yanked off her brown felt hat, folded it twice and shoved it into her overalls pocket. Just like she'd seen men do before they entered their own houses. Or if they stopped to have a word with their wives' friends in the street. Or when they reached the head of the soup-kitchen lineup.

While Nan dozed in Father's chair, Elsie peeled the spuds onto a sheet of newspaper. The pile of muddy skins had risen into a pyramid when she heard Ernest's signal. Three knocks. Never two or four. Always three.

That was something she could always rely on.

CHAPTER TWO

Ernest barged through the door without waiting for an invitation. He swept the door curtain aside. "You should hear this." His cheeks were flushed, his beady eyes shining. He leaned against the table, panting hard. "I heard. All about it. This afternoon. So I went. To investigate."

"Nan said to come back after supper." Elsie dropped another potato into the pot of water. "Did you eat already? What did you have?" Meals at Ernest's house were feasts compared to hers. The parents of his family's boarders often gave Mrs. Styles boxes of vegetables and fruit from their farms. Sometimes even meat.

"I couldn't wait, could I? I didn't want to get scooped. That's newspaper talk for having your idea pinched."

As she peeled the last potato in one long gray loop of skin, Ernest nudged her arm. The knife slipped, nicking her finger. "Watch out!" Elsie sucked at the bright bead of blood that welled up. She glared at him. "I've got chores, you know. Don't you?"

"Loads of them. I *am* the man of the house. But I got Gladdy to do them. This is real headline stuff." He tapped his notebook.

Gladdy was one of Ernest's four sisters; he called them the Noises. They and the boarders nagged and petted him so much that he often came to Elsie's to escape.

Ernest's father hadn't run off like hers. He'd just died.

"So what's this news, then?" She wrapped the newspaper around the potato peelings and shoved the bundle into the bucket under the table.

"Two nights ago, Branscombe's warehouse disappeared. Just like that! You know, the big one down by Main Street?" Elsie could almost count Ernest's freckles, he was standing so close.

"It was there one day," he said, "and gone the next." He looked at her as proudly as if he'd made the building disappear himself. "What do you think of that, then?"

"Warehouses don't disappear," Elsie said. "Maybe there was a fire. Or a sinkhole. I read about them. I bet the ground just opened up and swallowed it."

Ernest bounced up and down, his hair flapping and his freckles blurring. "No. No. That's not it." He'd have shaken his clothes loose if they hadn't already been untucked.

"Don't wake Nan!"

Ernest leaned toward Elsie and whispered, "I spoke with the authorities. The hoboes came. And they took it away." He nodded once and tucked his book in his pocket.

"Reverend Hampton's hoboes?" asked Elsie.

"Maybe not *his* hoboes, exactly," said Ernest. "But some bums. They stole that warehouse clean away in the dead of night. And you know the best part?" Now he sounded more like a little boy with candy than a newspaperman with an important story. "They took it apart, board by board, under cover of darkness. And you'll never guess what they used it for? Go on. Go on."

"Give me a chance." Elsie peered at Nan, whose head was tipped against the scratchy wing of Father's chair. A shiny drop of spit hung from the corner of her mouth. "A boat to sail on the Pacific Ocean?" suggested Elsie. "A stage for tap dancing?"

"You're not trying. Guess again!"

Elsie yanked her hat out of her pocket and jammed it on her head. "Okay. I give up."

"They used it to build a new shantytown. Halfway across town," said Ernest. "Overnight. Just like that!

That's what I heard. Let's go and see if it's true. We should go now, before the story goes cold."

Before Elsie could ask how a story could go cold, a voice came from behind them. "You're not going anywhere, Little Bit. Not until we've had our supper. And guess what I brought home for us all?" Elsie's uncle stood at the doorway, holding a bulging paper bag.

Ernest had been making such a racket, they had not heard Uncle Dannell and Dog Bob come in. "Don't call me Little Bit. I told you," Elsie said as a wet nose nudged her hand.

The scruffy black and white mongrel gave her a lick with his long tongue. Then he did the same to Ernest. "Gedoff!" he said. He shoved his hand in his pocket.

Dog Bob slumped down under the table with a sigh. He used to belong to Uncle Dannell's friend Bob, who had jumped a train to Calgary to look for work and hadn't come back. Dog Bob hardly seemed to miss his namesake.

Short and wide, Uncle Dannell had a huge smile just like Father's. A thin mustache crawled above his top lip like a dark worm. Father had a mustache too, although his was shaggier.

But Elsie was not going to think about that now.

"I expect your mother will be wanting you home," Uncle Dannell told Ernest. "It getting dark and all. How about you meet us at the end of the block.

Tomorrow first thing. We'll all go see this hot story that's going to get your name in the *Vancouver Sun*."

"But Dannell…," said Elsie.

"*Uncle* Dannell to you, Little Bit," he said. "No ands, ifs or buts. Tomorrow is another day, and I have a supper here the likes of which you've not seen since a month last Wednesday. With leftovers for Dog Bob, if he's lucky." He held out a hand to shake Ernest's. "Good night. With your nose for news, we should call you Scoop. Now that Elsie no longer likes her nickname, we'll give *you* one."

"Scoop. I like the sound of that," Ernest said. He shook Uncle Dannell's hand. Then he licked the tip of his stubby pencil and scribbled in his book. "What time? I'll make a note of it." He looked up. "We should find a new nickname for Elsie too."

"Sidekick. Scoop and Sidekick. How'd you like the sound of that?" Uncle Dannell wiggled his eyebrows at them both.

"I ain't no one's sidekick," said Elsie.

"It's 'am not', not 'ain't,'" said her uncle. "Don't let your mother hear you talk like that." He opened the door and stepped aside for Ernest-who-was-now-Scoop to leave. "How's seven forty-five sound? Be off with you, now."

When Ernest-Scoop had gone, Uncle Dannell turned sharply, like a soldier on parade. He bent down to hold his bag close to Nan's ear, crackling the brown paper to wake her up. "Mother Nan. How's about a little supper, then?"

Nan rolled her head and opened her eyes. "Hmph. A pay packet would be nice. But whatever this is may have to do. Otherwise it's potatoes and greens again." She groaned as she stood up. "*Phh.* These old bones. Elsie, you done those spuds yet?" Nan frowned at the bag Uncle Dannell had dumped in the middle of the table. "You look, Elsie," said her grandmother. "I wouldn't touch that object with a barge pole until I know what's inside. I know this fella's tricks. And take off that hat, child! How many times!"

CHAPTER THREE

Next morning, after a breakfast of toast and weak tea, with a slab of cold porridge in her pocket for lunch, Elsie trudged along beside Uncle Dannell and Dog Bob on their way to meet Ernest. She was going to have to get used to calling him Scoop. He'd been her best friend ever since she beat him at skipping stones at the tugboats hauling their loads down at False Creek. Katy Lillis and Ruth Cohen were her friends too. But you wouldn't catch *them* standing in black sticky mud under the Connaught Bridge, lobbing rocks with cold fingers.

Ruth and Katy were fine once in a while for looking through the Eaton's catalog with. Or playing jump rope or five stones. But Ernest—Scoop—always had real adventures in mind, always on the trail of a good story.

He'd told Elsie she could be his best friend until she grew nubs like the Noises. Until then, she was just as good as a boy, he said.

Elsie checked her chest regularly. But there were no sign of nubs yet.

Her fingers found the cold porridge in her pocket. If she ate it now, she'd have nothing for a snack at recess. "That was a lovely supper last night, wasn't it?" she said to Uncle Dannell. There had been just enough meat on the two chicken legs for the four of them, cooked up with Elsie's potatoes and the vegetables that Mrs. Tipson had passed on to them. Vegetables that came from what used to be Elsie's family's garden. But last night she had been too hungry to care.

There was even enough leftover gravy to dribble over Dog Bob's supper of stale bread.

"That was nothing!" said her uncle. "Just a little treat. By the end of the week, I will be in a position to treat us all to supper at Melvin's."

"How?" Elsie trailed her fingers across the fur on Dog Bob's back as he clicked along the sidewalk beside her. She often stopped by Melvin's Café on her way home from school. Not to go in. Just to peer through the steamy windows, to breathe in the lovely smell of bacon and coffee that wafted though the grille above the door.

Uncle Dannell reached inside his jacket and pulled out his oilcloth baccy pouch. He rolled a cigarette as he walked. "I have a brilliant idea," he said. "A failsafe plan, if I do say so myself."

"Can I help? Ern—Scoop and me are both good at schemes. They don't always work, but no one gets hurt."

Uncle Dannell snorted. "Sounds like something your Nan might say. But mustn't talk ill. Not many other people would take me in like that. Not after what my no-good brother did to you and your mother." He tucked his pouch back in his jacket. "But let's not be gloomy. My scheme, you may wish to know…"

But Elsie wasn't listening. Instead, she watched an old man muttering to himself as he leaned against a lamppost. He bent over and shoved a handful of newspaper into his boots. He wore a hat too, but his was stained, and ragged on one side. Not as nice as hers. He pulled it down low over his eyes like she did though.

Most of the hoboes never looked at you, Elsie realized. Not straight on. So as she passed him, she said, "Good morning, sir," to see what would happen.

Instead of answering—which would have been the polite thing to do—the man just lifted his other foot and shoved more newspaper into that boot before he pulled his trouser leg down as far as it would go.

Which wasn't far. His thin ankles stuck out like gray sticks above his boots. It looked like he got his clothes from the church rummage, just like she had to these days.

"...and it'll be a breeze." Uncle Dannell stopped to wait for Elsie and Dog Bob, who was doing his business against a wall covered in torn posters. "If I sell forty tickets, that's fourteen dollars' profit," he told her. "No problem. Don't you think? Now, where is that boy?"

They looked around, but there was no sign of Scoop. "Where is this place Scoop talked about, anyway?" asked Elsie. "If I'm late to school, Miss Beeston will give me lines."

"Did you hear a word I said?" Dannell asked. "I'm not used to being ignored. Oops. There he is." He grabbed Elsie's hand. "Here we go." With Dog Bob scuttling behind, he hauled her between the few cars lined up along the sidewalk, and then across the road and over the railroad tracks on the other side.

CHAPTER FOUR

Uncle Dannell didn't often run. He was panting hard by the time they reached Scoop, who was leaning against a broken wooden crate. He scribbled busily in his notebook, then closed it with a snap and stuck the pencil behind his ear. "See that?" He waved one arm. "All that wood and stuff there was part of Mr. Branscombe's warehouse just yesterday. Now it's a shantytown. Or will be when those shackers have done."

Wooden planks and sheets of corrugated metal had been used to build a jumble of shacks and lean-tos. Mountains of rusty old car parts rose between them. A huddle of men stood around a big black kettle balanced on a blazing fire.

Elsie watched a man crawl out from a hole between teetering piles of wood. He stretched and scratched and looked around as he joined the others at the fire. He held something on a stick above the flames.

"Squirrel for supper, do you think?" said Uncle Dannell. "Or rabbit?"

Elsie swallowed hard as Dog Bob trotted toward the men, drawn by the greasy smell rising from their fire.

Uncle Dannell quickly called to him. "Good boy. You stay here." He gave Dog Bob a quick pat when he came right back. "The survival instinct of those fellas," he said, shaking his head. He waved one arm at the shantytown. "It's a marvelous thing, I don't think." He stubbed out his cigarette on the sole of his shoe and tucked the stub into his pocket.

Elsie studied the men as they worked. Some wore pants, shirts and suspenders. Others hunched down inside long coats or jackets that looked like they once belonged to old suits. They shoved things around, leaned one sheet of wood against another, tucked in a chunk of cardboard, moved a rock to hold something else in place. A bunch of them shared a cigarette, passing it back and forth as they shifted from one foot to another, their shoulders pulled up to their ears.

Suddenly Elsie spotted a man in a long black coat near the back of the new shantytown. "There's Reverend Hampton."

Uncle Dannell and Scoop turned to look where she was pointing. "Busy as ever, your Nan's friend," said Dannell. "Out among his people. Silly bugger. 'Scuse my language." He spat on the rubble at their feet.

"Why silly?" Elsie asked.

"Who's he?" asked Scoop, his question falling on top of Elsie's.

Uncle Dannell answered them both at once. "The very Reverend Hampton tends to his flock by supporting schemes like this—a shantytown jury-rigged from a stolen warehouse. He can't just stick to his breadlines and soup kitchens. Oh, no. He tends to men who've abandoned their families and now only care about themselves." When Uncle Dannell scuffed his boot savagely on the ground, Dog Bob backed out of the way. "My brother is somewhere out there"— Uncle Dannell's voice was getting louder—"though heaven knows where he's skulking." His cheeks were bright pink now. His eyes flashed.

Elsie had heard him talk like this often enough. Nan called it "getting aerated."

And he hadn't finished yet. "*My* brother. *Your* father. Just as bad as this lot." He prodded one yellowed finger into Elsie's chest. "But don't you worry." Now he stabbed his own chest with his finger. "*I* will take care of my family even if your no-good father won't. You can rely on that."

Elsie thought she should defend Father. But what Uncle Dannell said was true. Her father *had* left them.

Maybe now he was just another shacker in another shantytown somewhere. Maybe he had already forgotten all about his family stuck living in a garage behind what used to be their own house.

And she was confused about what her uncle said about the Reverend. Surely it was good to want to take care of people? The Reverend came by to visit Nan most days and was always kind. He got aerated sometimes too. Talking about unemployment and people who could no longer afford a doctor. And children with not enough to eat. He had strong views about the System and Society—whatever they were. He said it was his job to help all God's children. That made sense to her.

"And now the latest," said Uncle Dannell. "You'll have heard all about it. The man's all set to shut down the dance marathon."

He flapped his arms around him to keep warm, and Elsie moved away so she wouldn't get hit by his big meaty hands.

"He spouts all kinds of rhetoric from the pulpit," Uncle Dannell went on. Nothing could stop him now. "Banging on about degradation and humiliation. When people are just trying to make a bit of money. He offers the hand of charity to his hoboes. No questions asked. But a dance marathon that might allow a few poor folks to make a few bucks?

Oh, no! We can't have that!" He pulled up his collar and stuck his hands in his pockets. He was silent for a long time while Elsie and Scoop watched the men in the shantytown pouring tea into tin cans.

"But enough of this," said Uncle Dannell. "We came, we saw. Now let's skedaddle. Come on, you lot. You're going to be late for school."

He turned around and started walking, slapping his leg to bring Dog Bob to his side.

What's a dance marathon? Elsie wanted to ask Scoop. *What's rhetoric? What's degradation?* But he had grabbed her arm with his bony hand and was hurrying her away as he ran to keep up with Uncle Dannell. "Did you interview someone?" she asked Scoop when they'd caught up. "Before we got there?"

"No one would say a word," he told her. "Because I'm just a kid, I bet. But when I'm famous? They'll be lining up to talk to me." He patted the bib of his overalls, where he'd tucked his notebook. "How about we find out more about these dance marathons your uncle was on about? After school?"

School! There was a spelling bee today. And Elsie had not practiced one word. "Did you study your list?" she asked Scoop, skipping over a big puddle.

His hands were in his pocket as he kicked a stone along the street. "Sure I did," he mumbled.

Elsie didn't believe him. Anyway, it wouldn't make a difference. Scoop, the newspaperman, was the worst speller in class. Probably in the whole school.

Elsie got top marks for spelling, but Miss Beeston kept her behind after school for sticking her tongue out at Jimmy Tipson when she should have been making a list of rivers of the world.

Scoop only got two out of twenty on his spelling test. He had to copy each word out thirty times before he was allowed to go. So it was nearly dark by the time they were let out of school, and they both had to go straight home.

CHAPTER FIVE

The next afternoon Elsie helped Scoop paint his mother's summer kitchen. It was his job as man of the house, he'd explained to Elsie. And the Noises were afraid of getting paint on their clothes. He knew Elsie didn't much care if her clothes were second-hand, too small or covered in paint.

It was Friday before she and Scoop had the chance to go looking for the dance marathon. They walked halfway across town, asking directions from two newspaper vendors, a policeman, a lady with a little kid hanging on to each arm, and a big man rolling barrels into an alley.

Scoop was pink in the face and panting, and Elsie's shoes were rubbing by the time they finally stood on Main Street in front of a rickety building that had once been a garment factory. Big white letters saying *Taylor's Clothing* still ran sideways up the brick wall.

While Scoop checked the back door for a way to sneak in, Elsie studied the billboard propped on the sidewalk. In the picture, a man in a dark suit and a bow tie and a woman in a long slinky evening gown danced together under a big glittering ball of mirrors. They smiled, showing bright teeth, as showers of light fell like silvery rain all around them. The words beneath the picture read:

DANCE MARATHON
Starts Monday!
Thirty Couples Dancing for Thirty Days!
Admission: 10¢ before 6pm; 25¢ after 6pm.
Winners Take All!
$1000 Prize!

"Does that really say one thousand dollars?" asked Elsie when Scoop came back. "That's a lot of money."

He took a quick glance at the billboard. But instead of answering her question, he just said, "It's locked up tight. I knocked, but no one answered."

"It's ten cents to get in," she told him.

"How much have you got?" Scoop stood with his hands in his pockets, his notebook tucked in the crook of one arm. The pencil propped behind his ear looked like it might fall any minute.

"Uncle Dannell told me he'd give me a dime for my spelling test. Let's come back on Monday when it starts. Now we know how to get here."

"Ask your uncle for two dimes," said Scoop.

"Get your own. Or ask your mom. Or the Noises."

"Fat chance!"

Fat chance? Maybe it didn't really matter if Scoop couldn't spell. He knew all the best expressions. Surely this was enough to make him the perfect newspaperman.

"Maybe Mother will let me have a dime for you too," said Elsie. "Mrs. Tipson paid her for cleaning their bathroom. What used to be *our* bathroom, before we got stuck in the garage." She crunched up her face. "Now we just have that stinky outhouse."

"You can use *our* bathroom anytime," said Scoop grandly.

Elsie looked at the billboard again. "We'll get twenty cents by Monday. Somehow. Come on. I'll catch heck if I'm late for supper." She walked away along the sidewalk.

Scoop didn't follow right away, so she turned back and grabbed his jacket sleeve to lead him down the street. He was too busy scribbling in his black and white book to look where he was going. Elsie had seen him walk into a lamppost or someone else on the street more than once. "Come on!" She peered sideways to read Scoop's notes about the dance hall.

She knew he always wrote very small so he would not be "scooped," and so the book would last a long while. His spelling was bad. His handwriting was awful too. Elsie couldn't make out a word.

CHAPTER SIX

Elsie could hear the ruckus when they were still half a block from home.

When Nan yelled, her voice warbled. Uncle Dannell's voice was a low rumble. And Mother sounded like a cat with its tail caught in a door. Elsie couldn't make sense of any of it. All she could hear were lots of words all jumbled together.

Scoop broke into a trot. "Let's check this out."

"Wait up." Elsie grabbed his sleeve.

The words were just starting to make sense. "Big chancer." Nan's voice. "Can't be trusted farther than I can throw you." Nan again.

"Oh, Dannell. Really!" It was Mother's voice this time.

"Will you let me speak?" Uncle Dannell suddenly shouted.

"That's some argy-bargy," said Scoop, ready to turn onto her street. He was just curious, Elsie told herself. Like any top-notch news reporter would be. But you kept family business to yourself, Mother always said. And this sounded like family business, all right. "Better not," she told him. "I'll see you tomorrow at the corner, like we agreed."

"You sure? Could be important." Scoop scuffed the ground with one boot as he looked hopefully in the direction of the shouting.

Elsie gave him a hard nudge with her elbow. "Go on. I'll tell you everything tomorrow."

"All right, all right. I'm going. If you promise." He stuck his tongue out at her and walked slowly in the direction of his own house. "I wanna know everything, mind," he called back to her as she headed home.

Uncle Dannell stood in the doorway looking at Nan and Mother, who had been doing the wash outside in the old tub. Nan's sleeves were rolled up to her elbows, and her hands were red and puckered. Mother's hair was in a roll on top of her head. Wet strands hung down by her face.

"Go inside," she said when she spotted Elsie at the end of the driveway.

Elsie would have liked to do as she was told. Dog Bob would be shivering under Uncle Dannell's bed.

He never liked loud voices. Nor did she. But she wanted to know what was going on, so she dragged her feet as she came up the path.

"Didn't I say to go inside?" said Mother, doing up the top button on her shirtdress. "Oh, what's the point? You might as well know. Your uncle. My precious brother-in-law." Her voice came out like a slow drip from a rusty tap. "He thinks he's clever. Too smart for his own good…"

"Bugger in a bag. That's what he is now and always was." Nan did not swear, not in the usual way. But she had a few special phrases she kept for really important occasions.

"Mother?" Elsie pulled up her socks as she watched her mother's face.

"Your uncle. We rely on him. It's hard without your father…We rely on Daniel." Mother retied her apron tightly and wiped her face with one hand.

Elsie knew this was serious. No one ever called her uncle by his real name.

"Now this," Mother continued. "We have to eat somehow. With four mouths to feed. A few hours next door is not enough…" She held a wadded handkerchief to her mouth, as if she needed to hold back other words that might come out.

Nothing made sense to Elsie. "Uncle Dannell? What did he do?"

"Your precious uncle…no relative of mine, mind…"
Nan's voice was cold and flat now, far worse than
her yelling. "Your uncle raffled his pay packet. Your
mother needs shoes if she's to keep looking for work.
You need feeding if you're going to learn anything.
But the big man here? A fortnight's work—the first
work in months—and he raffles his pay packet. Go on,
Mr. Big Ideas. Let's have no secrets here. How much
did you make on this scheme? Break this child's heart
too, why don't you?"

"It was fail-safe," said Uncle Dannell. "I explained
it all. Remember?" He was still leaning in the doorway.
But now he was looking down at the ground with his
hands shoved into his pockets. "It worked for Jamie
Mackenzie. He came home with forty-two dollars from
raffling his twenty-nine-dollar pay. Thirteen dollars'
profit. Seemed like a good risk. Don't you think?"

Elsie knew about raffles, sure. You took a chance
and paid a penny for a ticket. You might win something worth a nickel. Or even a dime. But raffling a pay
packet? "So what happened?" she asked.

Mother sniffed and patted back her hair. Elsie
noticed how thin she was. Her eyes had dark shadows
around them. "Your uncle sold tickets for a dollar
at the Fraser Arms," she told Elsie. Her voice now
just sounded tired and sad. "He sold seven tickets.
On a sixteen-dollar payday."

Elsie couldn't work out the math in her head; she was better at spelling.

"If they'd given me one more night, I could have made up the rest," said her uncle. "But the rule at the Fraser Arms is one night only. And they draw just before they close up. It was a quiet night, see? But rules is rules. I respect that."

"Oh. So you do respect something, do you?" said Nan. Instead of waiting for an answer, she shoved the wooden rollers off the washtub, heaved it onto its side and let the scummy water trail down the sidewalk.

Usually Uncle Dannell emptied the tub and put it away for her on wash day. But today Nan did it with her back to him, wrestling it onto its side and propping it against the wall.

"Fair and square, you could say," said Uncle Dannell. "Last week Edward Hooper took home twenty-four dollars for the price of a dollar ticket." But he didn't sound so sure of himself anymore.

"His family must have been glad of that," said Mother quietly.

It seemed a long time since Mr. and Mrs. Hooper had sat around in the front room with Elsie's family. They used to gather on Saturday nights to play whist and listen to Bing Crosby on the brown radio that sat on the sideboard under the mirror.

In Elsie's old home. Where Jimmy Tipson lived now.

"And you came home with eleven dollars for two weeks' work." Nan pushed Uncle Dannell out of the way with her elbow and disappeared into the garage. "Shame on you."

Dog Bob came out of the house as soon as Nan disappeared inside. In goes Nan. Out comes Dog Bob, thought Elsie. Just like the weather dolls in the clock that used to hang on the wall of Father's store.

Uncle Dannell's dog wandered from person to person. When no one petted him, he slunk out of sight around the corner.

It was okay for Dog Bob to disappear, thought Elsie. But she had nowhere to go. For a moment she was tempted to run after Scoop. Go home with him, where she was always welcome.

But this was family business. Her business. She would have to stay and see how it all turned out, whether she wanted to or not.

CHAPTER SEVEN

"What will we do?" Elsie asked. "What will we do for money if Uncle Dannell raffled it all away?"

Mother's thin hip pressed against Elsie's shoulder as she drew her against the damp warmth of her dress. "We'll think of something. It shouldn't be your problem." Her thin hands slid up and down Elsie's back. She smelled of soap and cooking fat; she used to smell of talcum and peppermints. It had been a long time since there had been candy in the house, and the lilac talcum powder Father bought Mother for Christmas had run out long ago.

When Elsie peered under her mother's arm, she could see Uncle Dannell crouched down against the wall. He was rolling a cigarette. He licked the edge of the paper and sealed it, then turned it between his lips and lit it with a match he pulled from a matchbox in one smooth movement. As he drew on his cigarette and held it away to watch the smoke that rose in the air, Elsie could tell he was trying to figure out what to say.

Mother was turned toward the street, looking at nothing.

"Would you believe I'm sorry?" asked Uncle Dannell finally.

Mother sighed.

If it's not one thing, it's another. That's what Nan would say, Elsie thought as she stood in her mother's arms, enjoying her warmth against her in the cool afternoon.

Nan's voice suddenly came from the doorway behind them. "Daniel Miller!"

Elsie's grandmother was rolling her sleeves back down, buttoning her cuffs. "Daniel. You have three days," she said. "Find a job. You'll make up that nine dollars. Or you are not welcome in this house." She pushed back her hair. "And that dog of yours neither."

Uncle Dannell didn't answer. He just looked at Nan for a minute before he turned back to Elsie and Mother. When nobody spoke, he threw down his cigarette butt without salvaging the leftover tobacco for later and trudged off down the path without a word.

Dog Bob emerged from behind the house, his ears flat against his head. He followed Uncle Dannell along the street as Nan turned away and disappeared into the garage again.

"No use standing here," said Mother. She took Elsie's hand and led her indoors. "I'm having a lie-down. I'm just not up to this." Nan was sitting in Father's chair, knitting fast and furiously. She didn't look up when they came in.

"Shall I brew up a cuppa?" asked Elsie.

"Makes no never mind to me," said Nan. "This floor needs a sweep though."

There was nothing wrong with the floor that Elsie could see. But after she'd put the kettle on to boil, she took the broom from its hook on the back of the door and gave the worn linoleum a lick and a promise.

As she turned to hang the broom back up, she saw a penny peeking out from underneath Father's chair. She picked it up and quickly tucked it in her pocket. If Nan saw it, she'd make her put it in the jar on the dresser.

A penny wouldn't go far. It wouldn't make up for what Uncle Dannell had lost with his pay-packet raffle. But with only nine cents to go, Elsie might soon have enough to get into the dance marathon. She knew better than to ask anyone for money now. Perfect marks on the spelling test, or not.

Uncle Dannell finally came home, just in time for supper. He'd found a *Columbian* newspaper on the street. Elsie could tell someone else had already read it. The front cover had been torn off, and a big black footprint covered the back page. It didn't look any different than the *Vancouver Sun*, Elsie thought. But Scoop turned up his nose at the *Columbian* when he passed the vendor on the street. His dad had worked for the *Sun*, which Scoop said always had much more exciting news.

Dannell spread the newspaper across the table and carefully read all the want ads, muttering under his breath, but not really directing his words to anyone in the room. Elsie saw him circle something with a nub of pencil. But before she had a chance to ask what it was, he ripped the page out, tucked it in his back pocket, and slipped the rest of the paper into his coat hanging on the door. It was probably a job ad, thought Elsie. Her uncle would soon get more work to make up the money he'd lost, and then maybe Nan would let him—and Dog Bob—stay.

At supper, even though Nan gave Uncle Dannell the smallest serving, he didn't say a word. He wouldn't even look at her. Everyone ate without speaking.

Elsie did the dishes in the yellow enamel pan on the table, then sat down to finish her math homework.

Once she'd got through the fractions Miss Beeston had set, she made a few calculations of her own on the back of her school scribbler.

There had been four of them when they first moved into the garage: Father, Mother, Nan and Elsie. Then Father disappeared. Leaving three. With one-quarter of the family missing, three-quarters were left.

Then Uncle Dannell came to stay. Four plus one equals five. Or would have been five if Father had still been there. So five people in the family minus Father was one-fifth missing.

So now there were four-fifths of the family living in the garage.

Elsie scratched her nose with the end of the pencil. It didn't make sense. Four-fifths was more than three-quarters. There was more of the family left now than when Father was there. But it felt like less.

Stupid math!

Elsie bit down hard on her lip so she wouldn't cry. She licked the tip of her pencil like Scoop did whenever he was getting ready to make some important notes. She tried a whole bunch of other calculations, but the numbers came out wrong every time. With people coming and going, there would never be enough left to make a whole family. What good were fractions?

Elsie dug an eraser out of the drawer and scrubbed at the paper so hard she almost rubbed right through.

She tore out the page and threw it into the pail by the door. And she didn't mention the family fractions when Mother checked her homework.

Maybe if Scoop wrote it all down in his notebook, as if it was one of his mysteries that needed solving, maybe he could make some sense of it.

To make herself feel better, Elsie took Mother's copy of *A Child's Garden of Verses* down from the shelf. The cover was stained and frayed in one corner, and the pages were soft as washed cotton from having been turned so often. Father used to read the poems at bedtime when she was little. Just before he tucked her in and kissed her good night.

The only sound in the room was Elsie flipping the pages, until Dannell said, "Fancy a walk around the block a time or two, Peg? I, for one, find it a bit close in here."

"I could use a bit of air," said Elsie's mother.

"Can I come?" Elsie closed the book.

"This is grown-up time, kiddo." Her uncle put on his jacket and tucked his newspaper under his arm. "Keep your nan company. We'll have us a round or two of cribbage when we get back. Ready, Peg?"

"Can I look at your jewelry box?" Elsie asked her mother. It was kept in an old nubby brown suitcase under the bed with Elsie's baby mug and her mother's scrapbook.

"Just make sure everything goes back in," said her mother. "And put that book away carefully. Your nan and grandpa gave me that when I was younger than you are now."

"You've told me that a million times," muttered Elsie, ignoring the look her grandmother gave her as they watched Mother tie her cardigan around her shoulders and change into her street shoes. The heels were all worn down; one sole flapped loose as she walked. "We won't be long," Mother said.

Dog Bob followed her mother and uncle out of the garage, wagging his tail madly.

Nan kept on knitting in Father's chair. She didn't look up or say a word as Mother and Uncle Dannell left the house.

CHAPTER EIGHT

As soon as the door closed, Nan set her tangle of wool and needles on the arm of the chair. She rubbed her crooked fingers and watched Elsie dump the contents of her mother's jewelry box onto the table. "Less and less in that thing all the time," Nan said. "Not much left to hock."

Elsie scrabbled through the old buckles and buttons. She studied Father's Tarzan candy cards and fingered the three old pennies Nan had brought with her from England, one so worn that it was hard to make out the face on the coin. She unfolded the tissue paper that held all her baby teeth. Even tooth fairies were out of work in the Depression, Uncle Dannell had said.

Elsie tucked the teeth back in the paper and took out Mother's mauve enameled flower brooch. She pinned it to her shirt collar, ducking her chin so she could see it.

"It's a crime, that," said Nan, her knitting needles clicking again.

"What is?" asked Elsie.

"Your father a jeweler. And that the only pretty thing your mother still has."

Elsie unpinned the brooch. "Is it valuable?"

"Some things are worth more than money can buy," said Nan. She held the needle of knitting in front of her and counted the rows with one finger.

How could something be worth more than money could buy? Elsie wondered as she polished the brooch with her mother's apron and put it back in the box. She arranged the Tarzan cards with her favorites on top and went through the buttons one by one, trying to remember which clothes they had come from. For a moment, she considered taking the English pennies to Mr. Archer at the bank. Maybe she could exchange them for enough Canadian money to get into the dance marathon. But when she imagined Father's voice saying *If you have to steal, it's not worth having*, she put them away.

Her uncle and mother came home just as she was locking the box again. Uncle Dannell helped Mother out of her cardigan. "Shall I brew up?" he asked.

Nan looked at him sharply. It was very unusual for him to make the tea. "Don't mind if you do," she said. "Where have you been?"

"There and back to see how far it is," he said. He winked at Elsie.

Nan harrumphed and frowned up at Mother, who looked away as Nan returned to her knitting. The sweater was the color of mud; Elsie would have preferred moss green. But another thing Nan often said was *We can make do by making do*. This didn't make any sense either, if you listened to it too closely. But Elsie knew what it meant. They all made do by making do these days.

"Everything back in one piece?" Mother reached across the table for the box. Elsie felt herself blushing. She nodded, feeling guilty about even thinking of stealing the money. She fetched the cribbage board from the cabinet next to Father's chair and opened the box of playing cards. They were soft with age. She rubbed her thumb against the little cigarette burn on the blue and white box, remembering how often she'd played with her father.

Where was he? Would he ever come home? How could her family fractions ever work out if he didn't?

The day Father left, he had gone out to apply for Relief. He'd done it before, but each time he had never got far. Once he got there too late, after he stopped in to visit a friend. Another time he got held up helping the coalman haul sacks off his wagon.

Mother had yelled at Father the time he said he'd run into the Reverend Hampton, who'd treated him to "tea and sympathy" at Melvin's, and got to the Relief Office too late again. That night she went to bed before supper and cried all night. Next day she hadn't said a word to Father or anyone else. Elsie thought that was the worst time of her life. Until the next day, when her father left home and didn't come back.

Nan and Mother had looked everywhere. They asked everyone they knew and inquired in the shops they regularly used. Nan even walked to the hospital and then made a nuisance of herself at the police station.

Mother had stayed in bed for four days when it looked as if Father had gone for good. Lots of men these days abandoned their families when times got tough. As if things would be easier without them. And she didn't get up again, except to go to the outhouse, until Mrs. Tipson asked her to come over to the house to bake a cake for Mr. Tipson's birthday. (Mother's baking was famous in the days the church ladies got together to talk about their charity work. But she didn't bake for her own family anymore, without an oven in the garage and no money for the ingredients.)

When she had come home that afternoon, Mother brought a little fairy cake for Elsie, cutting off the top and making it into two little wings that she'd stuck onto the cake with pink icing. How long would it be before there was cake again for tea in this house? Elsie's mouth watered just thinking about it.

Uncle Dannell crumbled stale bread for Dog Bob's supper as he waited for the kettle to boil. Elsie spread the cards out in a fan across her fingers, but her hand wasn't wide enough, and they scattered on the table.

"Budge over." Uncle Dannell put the Brown Betty teapot, four cups and saucers, and the cracked yellow sugar bowl on the table.

"It's too late for that child to be drinking tea," said Nan.

Uncle Dannell ignored her, pushing a cup toward Elsie, who could hear Nan tut-tutting behind her. "Once won't hurt," said Uncle Dannell. He winked at Elsie again.

What scheme was he cooking up this time? Her uncle always looked like this when he was planning something, Elsie knew. And his grand schemes often blew up in his face. Like that daft raffle idea.

Elsie looked at her mother. She seemed, if not happy, at least calm, as she poured her own tea. What *had* they talked about on their walk?

Between hands of cribbage, Elsie watched Nan pour her tea into her saucer to cool, then slurp it up from there. She could just about stand it when her grandmother did this at home. But if she did it when they were out or had company, Elsie wanted to curl up into a little ball and hide under the table. Mother had explained it was an old English country habit, and she'd laughed when Elsie said that Nan wasn't English anymore. Even if she was old.

Elsie couldn't remember the last time Mother had laughed. But she was smiling now.

Elsie had a pair of sixes, a jack of spades, a ten of clubs, a seven of diamonds and a four of hearts. Not a very good hand. But it didn't matter if she lost or won. She loved the slow march of matchsticks around the cribbage board, the scoring fifteen-two, fifteen-four and one for his nibs. Her family never let her win the same way some grown-ups did when they played with kids. Father often said that learning to be a good loser was part of growing up.

"Have we got an Eaton's catalog?" Elsie asked as she put the game back in the cabinet.

"Planning your Christmas list?" The matchstick between Uncle Dannell's teeth bobbed up and down as he spoke.

"Miss Beeston wants us to bring them to school tomorrow," said Elsie. "Don't know why."

"It's underneath the bed," said Mother.

"You're welcome to it," said Nan. "Nothing there we can afford. And we've got enough newspaper for now." To save money, scrap paper hung from a hook next to the toilet in the outhouse. Which reminded Elsie that she should go before she got ready for bed. She didn't like ducking out around the corner and along the gravel path when she was in her pajamas.

As she sat in the smelly dark outhouse, with cobwebs dangling from the ceiling and little skitterings in the wall, Elsie thought about how everything kept changing. The Depression was bad enough. Father running off was worse. Now it looked like her uncle was working on another scheme. They always got him into trouble.

When would things get better?

CHAPTER NINE

Elsie came back indoors and said good night. Nan offered the side of her dry papery face for a kiss, and Uncle Dannell gave her a smacker that echoed across the room. Her mother held her face against Elsie's for a moment, then gave her a quick hug before she let her go.

Elsie pushed the curtain aside to go into the bedroom, with Dog Bob clicking along behind her. Without waiting to be invited, he jumped onto her bed. When she had undressed, put on her pajamas and climbed under the covers, the dog lay down against her back. She opened *Little Women*, which she kept under her pillow with Baby, the doll Nan had knitted her years ago. Baby had lost one eye, and Elsie had sucked one of her hands so much that the wool was stiff and matted.

She tucked the doll under the covers next to her and turned the pages of her book. Jo, the main character, was going to be a writer when she grew up. Why had *she* never thought of that? Or of being a newspaperman, like Scoop? If the Depression ever ended, maybe there would be enough jobs for Elsie *and* Scoop at the *Vancouver Sun*. Or they could be rival reporters if she got a job at the *Columbian*.

The idea made her smile.

Elsie read the last page of the last chapter of her book aloud under her breath. *"Touched to the heart, Mrs. March could only stretch out her arms, as if to gather children and grandchildren to herself, and say, with face and voice full of motherly and grandmotherly love, gratitude and humility, 'Oh my girls, however long you may live, I can never wish you greater happiness than this!'"*

Did happy endings only happen in books?

Elsie must have dozed off. She woke suddenly to find Reverend Hampton peering around the curtain. "You look cozy," he said. "I know it's late, but I wanted to say a few words. Can I come in?" Nan's friend was tall and thin, with a long droopy face that reminded Elsie of a dog. But she couldn't think which kind. Certainly not one like Dog Bob's, with his happy eyes and lolling tongue.

Tonight the Reverend's thin hands were empty. He usually carried his Bible, which was thick and bulging, the dark red leather cover bent and flaking. Little notes and lists were always jammed between the pages. Scoop's notebook reminded Elsie of the Reverend's Bible, but without the psalms and prayers.

"Your mother suggested I have a few words," he said. "If you're not too tired."

"Okay."

As he bent toward her, Reverend Hampton's long arms swung at his side like the pendulums of a grandfather clock. Then they came to rest on his bent knees, where his black coat flared out. "I noticed you at the shantytown on Terminal Avenue a few days ago," he said. "That was you, I believe?"

"The hoboes stole the warehouse and built the shacks with the boards and things," said Elsie, pulling herself up higher on her pillow.

"That is the story, I know." Reverend Hampton tucked his hands into his wide sleeves.

"My friend is a newspaperman," Elsie told him.

"I thought that was your uncle I saw with you."

"Uncle Dannell came too. But my friend Scoop? His real name is Ernest, but we call him Scoop now. He was on the trail of the story. So we went to investigate."

"I see. Yes. I'm sure he heard some very exciting stories," said Reverend Hampton. He looked around as if he thought a chair might have appeared suddenly. Elsie knew she should invite him to sit on the bed, but she didn't want to.

"I just wanted to suggest…" He cleared his throat. "As a friend of this family…I go at will amongst the men. They are my flock too, just as you are when I visit you here. I come and go in the shantytowns, where I am known. But it would be better—if you don't mind my suggestion—that you do not go there." His folded pale hands looked like pieces of white fish. "These are dangerous places. These men are God's children, of course. But some of them are ill, some are weak. There's desperation amongst them. And anger. Do you understand?"

Nan's friend kept talking, without waiting for Elsie to answer what she guessed Uncle Dannell would call a rhetorical question. The kind that's not meant to be answered. "I have spoken to your mother," Reverend Hampton said, "and to your grandmother. They agreed that I should speak to you. I hope I have not intruded."

Elsie shook her head. Then she nodded. She and Scoop had worked out a system long ago. If she was very careful not to actually *say* that she would not go to the shantytown again, she would not have promised anything.

The Reverend cleared his throat and smiled at her. "I'm glad we had this chat." He tugged on the lapels of his black coat and turned to go back into the other room.

Out of the blue, Elsie heard herself ask the question she'd wanted to ask for a long time but had not dared. "Reverend?"

He turned back. "Child?'

"If you ever see my father? Maybe in the shanty-towns. Or when you're working on the breadlines. We've looked. But we can't find him. He was going to the Relief Office, but they said he never got there. But if you do see him"—she took a deep breath—"will you tell him to come home?" Her throat was too thick to let any more words out.

"Oh, my child." Reverend Hampton cleared his throat. "Of course. You have my word. If I see your father, I will tell him that you need him."

Elsie felt the lump in her throat dissolve. She blinked and shifted down in the bed, pulling the covers up to her chin. "Thank you."

"You are most welcome. It would be my pleasure."

Elsie closed her eyes as the Reverend went through the curtain to join the grown-ups. She opened them again as she heard the voices coming from the other side of the curtain. The dance marathon! She should have asked Reverend Hampton about it. Maybe he could explain what was so bad about them.

She pulled Baby into her arms.

She and Scoop would just have to find out for themselves.

CHAPTER TEN

At school the next day, Elsie's class used their catalogs to calculate the cost of a spring wardrobe for a family of four. She couldn't imagine ever having that much money, or wearing those kinds of clothes again. Then they picked out furniture for their dream bedrooms and drew floor plans to see how it would fit in. Finally everyone cut out pictures they liked and glued them onto a long sheet of newsprint. Elsie, Jack Cattermole, Sheila Phipps, Roddy McPherson and Ruth Cohen were assigned to color a border around it to brighten up the collage. Miss Beeston planned to hang it on the back wall of the classroom.

"I can color just as well as any of that lot," Scoop told Elsie on the way home, as he kicked at anything that lay on the sidewalk. "I don't know why I wasn't chosen to do that border thing." He picked at the dried wallpaper paste on his fingers. "Anyway. It's a stupid idea. That collage will look like a dog's breakfast."

"Dog Bob has bread and water for breakfast. And dinner too. It won't look anything like it." Elsie flicked him with her hat.

"Don't be so stupid. You know what I mean."

"You can walk by yourself if you're going to be rude," she said.

"You sound just like your nan," said Scoop. "You're as pigheaded as she is." With that, he shoved his hands into the pockets of his overalls and strutted off around the corner.

"'Good riddance to bad rubbish,'" muttered Elsie. She kicked at a can, and it clanged as it thumped against the lamppost. When she chased after it and did it again, it wobbled into the road and stopped on a grating. She would have gone after it and given it one more mighty kick if she hadn't seen Mrs. Tipson headed toward her.

Elsie pulled her hat down tight and dashed off the other way, pretending she hadn't seen the lady who now lived in her old house.

"Where's that catalog?" asked Nan when Elsie got home and dumped her schoolbooks on the table.

"You said we didn't need it anymore."

Nan tutted. "Your mother wants you," she said. "She's in the bedroom."

Mother was folding clothes into the suitcase that usually held Elsie's baby things and her own jewelry box.

"Where are we going?" asked Elsie.

Mother carefully folded her minty green blouse and laid it on the bed. "My old friend Daisy Newman is very ill in New Westminster. She has no one to look after her."

Elsie had been to New Westminster once for the May Day parade. They had gone on the Interurban train, the only time she'd been on a train in her life. But she had never heard of this Daisy Newman. "When are we going?"

"I'm going alone," her mother told her. "You'll stay here with Nan and Dog Bob."

"How long are you going for?"

"A couple of weeks. Maybe a little more. We'll see."

Elsie hated *We'll see. We'll see* really meant *Maybe yes. Maybe no. Probably no.* It meant, *Maybe you'll forget what you've asked and I won't ever have to answer. We'll see* was always the wrong answer.

"Who's Daisy Newman, anyway?" Elsie asked.

"I told you. A school friend. We were very close."

"You never told me about her. Why can't I come? I don't want you to go."

Mother pushed the suitcase aside and sat down on the bed. She pulled Elsie toward her so she was standing between her knees. "You've got school.

And I'm only going away for a little while." She pushed a hair away from Elsie's face. "You'll be fine here with Nan. Things change, my love," she said. "But life goes on."

That was just the kind of thing Nan would say. Of course life goes on. What else could it do? Elsie leaned away from her mother's arms to poke through the things in the suitcase. "Why are you taking these?" Ivory dancing shoes peeked out from under an orange satin blouse with a floppy collar.

"Perhaps my friend and I will do a little dancing," Mother told her.

"I thought she was very ill," said Elsie.

Mother got up and pushed the bed back so she could get at the bottom drawer in the dresser. "Would you like to help me pack? If not, you might help your grandmother with the supper."

Elsie didn't want to do either. She wanted to dump everything out of the suitcase onto the floor. She wanted to fling the filmy blouse and the dancing shoes and her mother's good tweed skirt and cable-knit sweater across the room. She wanted to send her underthings into the air like rude birds. She wanted to demand that her mother stay here. With her and Nan and Dog Bob and Uncle Dannell. Father had gone. And now Mother was going away. The family fractions would change all over again.

Elsie felt just like Dog Bob, always circling around, trying to keep everyone where they belonged.

She wanted to kick the bed the way she'd kicked the can on the street. She wanted to stamp her feet and yell that it was not fair. But if she did, she knew she'd hear Nan's voice coming through the curtain: *If you think life should be fair, you've got another think coming.*

So Elsie sat on the bed and watched her mother pack. But she refused to help. And Mother had another think coming if she expected Elsie to speak to her for the rest of the evening, even though she was dying to tell her about the Eaton's catalog project, and the collage, and the fight she had with Scoop.

They were supposed to be best friends. But he wasn't talking to her, and she hadn't even grown nubs yet. What would it be like when she did? She wanted to talk to her mother about that too.

Elsie ate her supper slowly, feeling Mother's gaze on her. By the time she was done, she had decided the only thing to do was to be a good loser like Father had taught her to be. If she could be a good loser when he left, she could be one when Mother went away to visit a sick friend. "We did loads of things with the Eaton's catalog today." Elsie watched her mother's face brighten now she was talking to her again. "We furnished our dream bedrooms, and we made a collage too."

"Dream bedrooms, my eye," Nan muttered from her chair behind them. But no one answered her.

Later, Elsie won three games of checkers with Uncle Dannell while Mother washed the dishes. As she helped him put the little black and white pieces back in their box, Uncle Dannell said, "So, it'll just be you and your Nan for a while. Can I leave Dog Bob in your care?"

"What do you mean?" Elsie closed the box and held it against her chest. "Where will you be?"

Her uncle glanced over at Mother, who was hanging the damp dishcloth on the string overhead.

She turned sideways to look at Elsie, her hands still in the air, with clothespins between her fingers. "Didn't I mention it earlier? Your uncle has work." Mother picked up the laundry basket and hugged it to her chest. "In the cranberry fields at Richmond."

"A supervisory position." Uncle Dannell puffed out his chest and flicked his suspenders with a loud snap. Nan took the basket from Mother without saying a word and disappeared into the bedroom.

Elsie felt her chest fill up with heat. "You're going to New Westminster?" she yelled at her mother. "*And* Uncle Dannell is going to Richmond?" She tugged her hat down hard on her head, watching Mother take off her apron and fold it into a tiny square.

"You got it, baby girl," said Uncle Dannell.

Elsie didn't like his smarmy voice. Or being called baby girl. It was even worse than being called Little Bit. "Don't call me that. How many times do I have to tell you? Anyway. We don't have any money. How are you going to get there?"

Uncle Dannell looked at Mother. Mother looked at the floor and quietly said, "I pawned my brooch for my fare." She unfolded her apron again and smoothed it against her stomach. "Uncle Dannell will hitchhike. Don't worry…" She must have seen Elsie's eyes fill with tears at the thought of the last piece of jewelry from Father's shop being in the pawnshop for anyone to buy. "We'll get it back when Uncle Dannell has his first paycheck," she said.

Elsie rushed into the bedroom, where she found Nan sitting on the bed with her hands folded in her lap. Nan doing nothing!

Dog Bob was slumped on the floor beside her. He blinked up at Elsie.

"Everyone's going, Nan," Elsie cried. "I don't want them to go." She gulped and felt the tears flood her eyes.

"Nor me, my child." Nan ran her hand down Elsie's cheek, then pulled her into her wide lap. "Nor me." It had been a long time since Elsie had sat there.

Nan's chin came down on the top of Elsie's head and her voice rumbled through her skull. "But we all have to find a way to do the best we can. These are hard times, child, and everyone should do their bit. Your mother says her friend is well situated, so she'll have good food there, and there will be one less mouth to feed here for a while. Meanwhile, she can lend a hand to someone in need. Your uncle? Well, that one's another story. But he's got to bring some money into this house if he's to stay."

Elsie felt so tired. How could she ever get everyone to stay in one place long enough to be a complete family again? Just for the moment, sitting in Nan's lap was the best place to be in the world. She closed her eyes and followed the feel of her grandmother's hands as they stroked her hair and ran down her back. "The time will go quickly," Nan was saying. "Your mother will come home as soon as her friend is better. And we can hope that Daniel does nothing rash this time. A bit of farm work might do the man good." Just as Elsie thought she could fall asleep in her soft lap, Nan pushed her away. "No moping, now. You and I will be good company for each other. And this beast..." She gave Dog Bob a shove. "He's on my feet. Never mind my rheumatism. Come on, it's time you were in bed." Nan heaved herself up with a sigh and disappeared through the curtain into the living room before Elsie could say anything.

She changed into her pajamas very slowly and climbed under the covers. She needed to go to the outhouse. But she'd rather wet the bed than face Mother again.

CHAPTER ELEVEN

A few days later, Elsie and Ruth Cohen linked arms all the way home, chanting "Easy Ivy Over."

Maybe Ruth could be her best friend now that she and Scoop were on the outs. He'd trailed behind for a while, then cut up an alley when Elsie didn't answer after he'd called to them for the third time.

She was still mad at him for being such a bad loser and being so rude about the collage. It didn't look like a dog's breakfast; it was bright and colorful, hanging on the wall at the back of the classroom, behind the old cast-iron stove.

Ruth went home in a sulk after Elsie won three rounds of five stones. Maybe she was not best-friend material, thought Elsie as she sat on the cold sidewalk playing cat's cradle with some leftover yarn Nan had given her.

Dog Bob lay on the grass beside her, chewing the hair between his pads, making disgusting wet sounds and growling at himself.

Elsie looked up when she heard whistling behind her. Scoop skidded to a halt beside her. "What's happenin'?" He plopped down and folded his skinny legs under him. "You got over the hump?"

"You got mad first," she said. "Sulking! Just like crybaby Ruth Cohen."

"Did not!"

"Did so!"

Scoop grinned. "I'll quit if you'll quit." He held his curled hand toward Elsie, his little finger sticking out. She looked at it for a moment, then linked fingers with him. They shook.

"Enough is enough," said Elsie.

"Enough is enough," echoed Scoop. He thwacked her on the back, which she knew boys did instead of hugging.

It felt good to be friends again. Elsie picked up the five stones from the gutter. "Wanna play?"

Scoop brushed the stones from her open hand. "Dumb girls' stuff. I've got better things to do." He scratched the top of his head so his hair stuck up like a rooster's comb.

"I wish I did," said Elsie. "Nan wants me to stay close by until supper." She nodded toward the garage.

"She's spring cleaning. She's always cleaning or doing wash. It wears me out." She shuddered. "Anyway, I'm not going inside until Mother and Uncle Dannell come home. I just decided."

"Now who's got the hump? What about your supper? Hey. Did you get a letter yet?"

Elsie shook her head. Still no news from her father. And Mother hadn't yet written to let them know she'd arrived safely in New Westminster, or to say when she might be home.

"Aren't you just dying to know if she's dead or alive? Her friend, I mean?" asked Scoop.

"Do you think maybe Mother's never coming home? Like Father?" asked Elsie. "He never wrote either."

"Nah." Scoop didn't sound very sure of himself. "Maybe you just haven't exhausted all avenues. Trying to find your dad, I mean."

"Which avenues? We looked everywhere."

"Not those kind of avenues. It's reporter lingo for trying everything."

"When Nan went to the police, they said if they had to track down every man who left home without a word, they'd never catch the real criminals," Elsie told Scoop. "It's something to do with the times. Lots of men leave home without a word to anyone. He's not in the hospitals. Mother checked. And Uncle Dannell did too." Elsie bit hard on the inside of her lip to stop herself crying.

She had discovered this helped at night when she felt Nan's bulgy backside against her in the old iron bed, and only cold sheets and drafts on the other side, where Mother should have been.

"If you're going to cry, I'm going home," Scoop said. "One of the Noises' gentlemen friends has let her down—don't know how, no one will give me the details—but I get enough tears at my house. Don't you blubber on me, hear?" He nudged her hard with his bony elbow.

Scoop must have more bones than anyone she'd ever met, thought Elsie. They seemed to stick out long past where his body should have ended. At his shoulders. His knees.

Elsie hugged her knees. She could feel the rough gravel poking through the seat of her pants. "Nan pretends she's not bothered about Mother," she told him, "but each time the mailman's due, she finds something to do out by the Tipson's mailbox. Do you think Father wrote us a letter and they never passed it on? That Jimmy is so mean, I bet he'd do it. Do you think he's been hiding Mother's letter?" Elsie rested her chin on her knees and watched Scoop poke a stick in circles along the sidewalk. She looked at him sideways when he didn't answer. "Well? Do you?"

"Do I what?"

"You're not listening."

"What I was thinking was…we need to explore all avenues, like I said. So tomorrow? There's no school, so we can head out to that shantytown. Put the word about."

"What word? The Reverend said those places are dangerous. He said they're desperate, some of those hoboes. Though they looked okay to me the other day. Just rough maybe."

"I'll go then, if you're chicken," said Scoop. "I can do the investigating myself. If we find your father, maybe you won't mind so much about your mother."

Elsie stared at Scoop. Could he really think that as long as she had one parent at home, it wouldn't matter where the other was? Maybe it was easier for him—his father couldn't come home no matter how much anyone else wanted him to. Dead is dead and done for, as Nan would say.

Elsie felt a chill as soon as she thought the words. Surely she'd know. She'd feel it somehow, if Father was dead. Wouldn't she?

CHAPTER TWELVE

"I'll need a description." Scoop rooted around in his pocket for his pencil.

"You know what Father looks like." Elsie didn't want to admit that sometimes she could hardly remember her father's face. She took out a photograph from her back pocket and smoothed it against her knee. "I pinched this from Mother's suitcase. She'd packed it to take on her trip to New Westminster."

Scoop grabbed it. He peered at it and nodded. "This will do. Better than a description." He took his notebook from his overalls, opened it up and carefully laid the photograph between the pages.

Elsie could already feel the empty space where the picture had been. She'd got used to putting her hand in her pocket during the day, just to be sure the snapshot was still there. At night she stuck it under her pillow, then imagined she could feel it under her head all night, like the story about the princess and the pea. "I want it back, mind," she told him.

"Sure," said Scoop. "When the Reverend told you not to go to the shantytowns, what did you do?" he asked. He rolled up his trouser leg and picked at the edges of a scab on his knee.

"The magic nod," said Elsie. "That says I heard him. But no promises."

"That's the ticket. So you could come if you want to."

"What about Mother?"

Scoop flapped an arm in the air. "She's just in New Westminster, waiting for her friend to die. There'll be a letter soon." He rolled down his trouser leg and then looked up at her again. "Do you think it will be a long, slow, agonizing death?"

Elsie didn't say anything. It was another of those questions that didn't really need an answer.

She and Scoop sat with their feet in the gutter, flicking stones at the few cars that passed by. Even though they missed every time, it was almost as good as skipping stones on the river, where the tugboats steamed past dragging log booms. She would have suggested that they go down there now, but Nan had said to stay close to home. With Father gone, then Mother and Uncle Dannell, perhaps Nan wanted her close by for her own sake. Not for Elsie's. Besides, the Reverend Hampton was coming by after supper. Elsie had told him she needed some trousers; the ones she had were at least three inches too short for her already, and her ankles got cold on the way to school. He had promised to see what he could find in the church rummage. She would go indoors when the Reverend got here.

After Scoop and Elsie arranged to meet at the end of the block outside Lewis's Repair Shop the next morning, they practiced whistling. Scoop could only spit noisily. Elsie whistled "Yankee Doodle" right through without hardly taking a breath.

"What are you children doing sitting in the dirt?" Elsie turned to see Nan coming down the path toward them. "I've been calling you for supper, miss. Time for you to go too, young man. Get on with you."

"Where's the fire?" muttered Scoop. He leaned over to give Dog Bob a tummy tickle. Then he stood and hitched up his pants. He was the only person in the world who wasn't scared of Nan.

He said goodbye, then strolled down the road, his hands in his pockets, his elbows sticking out in triangles as he rocked from side to side. Nan laughed as she watched him go. "He's a case, that one. Come along now." She put one hand on Elsie's back as they walked toward the garage, Dog Bob trotting ahead of them.

"And that hat comes off as soon as you go inside," Nan told Elsie. "How many times!"

But Elsie wasn't listening. Uncle Dannell said that with the proper training, Dog Bob would have been the perfect sheepdog. Even without it, it was in his nature to try and keep everyone in his pack together. It had to do with instincts, he told her.

Maybe she had the right instincts for finding her father. If he was down in the shantytown with all the other hoboes, she would find him and bring him home.

As she waited for Scoop the next morning in front of Lewis's Repair Shop, Elsie studied the radios in the window. She ran her finger down the glass, then rubbed the black smudge off on her coat. She paced back and forth along the sidewalk, dodging out of the way when someone wanted to go into the shop. Dog Bob drifted off to sniff around, then came back and sat beside Elsie for a bit before leaving again.

After she had asked three passersby the time, Elsie figured Scoop wasn't coming. She checked the street one way, then the other, so many times she was almost dizzy. She could go over to his house. But if he was stuck at home doing chores, he'd want her to stay and help.

She did enough of them at home now that there was only Nan and her.

A streetcar rattled past with a boy hanging off the back, one arm and one leg stuck out in a V. He yelled as he passed, but she couldn't make out what he was saying. Scoop had tried that once. He'd ripped his pants and got a long gouge along his leg when he fell off. Try explaining that to Nan if *she* tried such a stunt, thought Elsie.

Checking one more time that Scoop wasn't coming, Elsie looked toward home once, and then she headed off in the direction of the shantytown alone. She stuck her hands in her pockets and stuck her elbows out like Scoop, to make herself feel brave. Dog Bob would keep her company, even if her best friend had left her high and dry.

The closer Elsie got to the shantytown, the fewer cars were on the road. There weren't many newspaper vendors about either. Or ladies with their shopping bags and high heels. Most of the storefronts Elsie passed were all locked up, with strips of wood making big Xs across the windows. Others had metal grilles and fat padlocks keeping them shut up tight. Two young men tottered past, leaning against each other as they gulped from a bottle sticking out of a paper bag. When one of them dribbled down his jacket, he pulled up the lapel to his face and licked it off.

Elsie moved closer to the shuttered storefronts. She looked straight ahead as she hurried on. Dog Bob kept up most of the time. When he strayed, she clicked her tongue, and he came back right away.

They were alone on the street now. Elsie really wished Scoop was with her, whistling and talking a mile a minute. But she was not such a chicken that she couldn't go alone to find her father.

CHAPTER THIRTEEN

Elsie stepped across the train tracks, kicking through the litter and old cans that drifted between the rails in the squally wind. The air was smoky; the stink of something sweet mixed with something bitter hung in the air.

Dog Bob followed the trail of garbage, his nose down low so he didn't miss a single smell. Soon he looked as small as a cat in the distance. He'd come back in a minute, Elsie thought. She pulled her hat down tight and buttoned her jacket all the way. She tried to walk with a Scoop-like swagger, but she needed her hands out now in case she tripped over the rubble. Her knees felt soft, as if there were no bones in them.

"What are you doing here?" A man had come out of nowhere. He stared down at her with damp red-rimmed eyes. His shoulders were tucked up high, almost to his ears. A tattered brown scarf was wrapped across his body.

"I'm looking for my father," said Elsie. She shoved her hands in her jacket pocket.

The man spat a long stream of tobacco juice onto the ground and stared at her.

"His name is Joe Miller," she told him.

"Half the guys here are called Joe. I don't know about no Miller."

"He's not very tall and not very short. He's a bit round. But not fat. He's got dark hair and brown eyes…"

"Hey, fellas!" When the man yelled, more hoboes emerged from nowhere. One of them almost tripped as he came toward them. They shuffled to stand around her in a circle.

"I'm…I'm just…I just wanted to know if you have seen my father," said Elsie.

"His name is Joe," said the first hobo. One side of his lip slid up higher than the other in an unfriendly smile.

Another man laughed, a harsh laugh that turned into a cough. He spat onto the ground and coughed again. "Joe! That should make it easy," he said.

When Elsie looked closer, she could see that one of the hoboes wasn't much older than Scoop. Even though his skin was not as bristly as the others', his face was just as red and chapped. Freckles ran all the way up his forehead and disappeared under his cap. He scratched his neck and stared back at her. "Seen enough?" he asked.

"I'm looking for my father." Her voice sounded thin.

"If he's here, he prob'ly don't want to be found," said the man who had tripped. He picked up a plank from the ground and leaned on it. "And if he's not here, you're in the wrong place." Before Elsie could step away, he reached forward and flipped her hat off her head.

"Hey!" She barely managed to grab it before the man did. She grazed her fingers as she pulled it up off the ground, getting a whiff of his dirty body as she did so. She turned her hat around in her hand to straighten it. She smacked it hard against her coat to get the dust off, then pulled it down hard on her head. "That's mine," she said, almost to herself.

The men still stood around her, not speaking.

Elsie's chest felt as if it had filled with ice. She knew she would cry if she stayed here much longer, surrounded by these dirty, unfriendly men. She didn't like the look in their eyes. Or their smiles. And she didn't like their silence.

She was just wondering how she was going to get away, when, in the distance, a man walked between the rows of shacks, pulling a dog along on a rope.

"Dog Bob!" Elsie took one step to run toward the man. "Hey! That's my dog!"

The other hoboes shuffled together to form a wall of smelly tweed and stained raincoats.

Peering between them, she could see Dog Bob pulling against the rope. "Here, boy!"

He pulled even harder when he heard her voice. But the man holding him yanked on the rope until Dog Bob's front legs were off the ground, his legs pedaling the air as if he was riding a bicycle.

Elsie looked from her dog to the men standing around her. Staring down at her, they eased closer together, not saying anything, making a barrier between Elsie and Dog Bob's kidnapper. Their hands were in their pockets, their chins tucked down into their chests.

"Give him back." Elsie's voice wobbled. "That's my dog."

One of the men leaned forward and stared right into her eyes. "Says who?" He spat. She stepped back as a slimy gob landed on her jacket. She wanted to say, *Elsie says. That's who.* That's what Scoop would have done.

The hobo who spat was still peering at her. And the others weren't lifting a finger to help her. She felt very small, and her legs were starting to get shaky. She took one step backward.

The men took one step toward her.

As Elsie took another step back, her foot caught on a chunk of stone. She felt her ankle twist as she stumbled to catch her balance.

The men stepped forward again. Bigger steps this time.

Elsie could smell smoke and sweat and a stink like rotten potatoes. In a sliver of light between the hoboes, she saw Dog Bob being hauled away by the man. But she felt frozen in place, with a chill creeping down her legs and up into her collar. The Reverend had been right. She shouldn't have come. With or without Scoop.

But then she thought of Dog Bob, always running back and forth trying to keep track of everyone. It was her turn now. If she didn't get Dog Bob back now, he might never come home. And what would she tell Uncle Dannell?

Elsie longed to be holding her uncle's meaty hand. She wished Scoop was here, jumping up and down with bright ideas and daring plans. But there was only her, with a bunch of dirty men staring at her, waiting to see what she would do next.

When a car horn suddenly blared from the road behind her, it was as if someone had poked Elsie with a sharp stick. "I want my dog!" she yelled. She looked into each man's face and hung onto her jacket lapels with both hands as she tried to make herself bigger and taller. "That's my dog. That's Dog Bob. And I want him back."

One man stepped away from the group. Another looked down at the ground and scuffed at something that wasn't there. The one who reminded her of Scoop muttered, "She's just a kid."

Behind them, Dog Bob was still pulling on the rope, his feet scrabbling in the dirt. He whimpered, and his nose was glistening.

Elsie used her elbows as if they were pointy and dangerous, like Scoop's, to shove past the men. She was surprised when they shifted away to make room for her. As she kept walking on her cold shaky legs, she sensed the men standing behind her, watching to see what she would do.

As Elsie got closer, the man holding Dog Bob's rope did not let go. But he didn't keep dragging the dog away either. He just stood there, looking over her head at the men behind her. She ran toward Dog Bob and dropped to her knees, gathering him into her arms. He trembled as he lapped her neck with his tongue.

"You are *my* dog," she said into his warm side. "And I won't go home without you." Then she lifted her head and looked at the hobo holding him. "This is *my* dog. I want him back." The man only had one eye.

The other was just a big bulgy lump under a flap of skin that went all the way down to his nose. Elsie looked away from him to where the men all stood in a silent huddle, waiting for her to do something.

She rubbed her chin in Dog Bob's bristly fur. Then she lifted her face and heard herself say something that Nan said all the time. Something she had never imagined coming out of her own mouth. "You should be ashamed of yourself," she told the man.

His good eye blinked.

Elsie liked the voice that had come out of her mouth. She sounded like someone who meant business. Even Dog Bob was listening to her, his head cocked to one side. "You should be ashamed of yourselves," she said again. This time when she yanked on the rope, it came loose in her hand.

The one-eyed man who'd stolen Dog Bob stepped back. He looked at the other men, who were all looking anywhere but at her, lighting cigarettes, mumbling to each other.

As Elsie stood up, Dog Bob was so close to her, she could feel his warmth against her leg. Holding his rope tightly in one hand, she turned to the men who were slowly moving away, their backs to her now, as if nothing had happened. "You should ALL be ashamed of yourselves!" she yelled. Her voice echoed through the alleys between the shacks.

These men, with their stubbly cheeks and grubby hands and trembling chins and shiny eyes, were all the things that the Reverend had said they were. They were angry and defeated and desperate. And the shantytown was not a safe place to be. She should not be here.

Elsie knew it now.

She held on tightly to Dog Bob's rope as she headed back toward the railroad tracks and the street beyond. If she let go, he would follow her home to make sure she got there safe and sound, because that was his job. He was so close to her, he could almost have shared her shoes.

But Elsie held on tight to her uncle's dog as she stumbled away on her rubbery legs.

Scoop had once told her that heroes show they are brave by walking away from their enemies without looking back. But Elsie knew the reason heroes don't look back—it's because they don't want anyone to know they're afraid.

She was so scared, she couldn't stop her teeth chattering.

But she had saved Dog Bob from the one-eyed man. She had got herself out of the scrape. And she still had her hat.

Elsie kept her back straight as, very carefully, watching every step, she put one foot in front of the other until she knew the shantytown was well behind her. Until she and Dog Bob had crossed the railway tracks. Until they had made it back onto the other side of the road.

Her breath was so hot in her chest, it felt like knives poking at her. Her ankle hummed with pain. Holding the rope tightly, with Dog Bob trotting along beside her, Elsie started toward home.

Because even heroes knew that home is always the safest place to be.

CHAPTER FOURTEEN

Still panting, her foot aching, Elsie slowed down to walk the last few blocks. She rubbed the front of her coat with a piece of newspaper she found stuck to a fence, and stamped her feet to get the shantytown dust off her boots.

When she got home, it was not even lunchtime. On the table were two soup bowls and spoons, with a cup and saucer at Nan's place and a glass at Elsie's. She gave Nan a long hug and waited until her grandmother let go of her before she stepped out of her arms.

"You sickening for something?" Nan touched Elsie's cheek with the back of her hand. "You are a bit flushed."

"I'm fine," she said. But she wasn't. She felt like a slice of bread with the middle chewed out. All empty and hollow, with her crust folding in on her.

"There's soup," said Nan. "But perhaps you should have some corn mush and hot milk." This was her cure for almost everything. Usually Elsie hated the feel of gummy cornmeal behind her teeth, the wrinkled skin on the warm milk. But suddenly that's what she wanted more than almost anything in the world. "Do we have currants?" she asked. "Can I have it in bed?"

Nan stood back and set her fists against her waist. "You do look peaky. You and Scoop been up to something?"

"No." It was the truth. Elsie had been up to something. But not Scoop.

"I thought he was with you. He gone home already?" asked Nan.

"Mmm." That wasn't a lie either. He must be at home. Or he'd have been at the shantytown with her.

Nan patted her apron. "All right then. You go tuck down. I'll be in with your bowl in a bit."

On her way to the bedroom, Elsie bent down to put her hand against Dog Bob's side. His heart thumped against her fingers, and his coat was damp and twitchy. He gave her a long, doggy look and dropped his head onto his front paws.

Elsie shucked off her coat and laid it across the foot of her bed. She took off her pants and sweater and climbed into bed in her underwear and socks.

She pulled the cold covers up to her chin. At night, the room was almost cozy with the flowery curtain down the middle of the room and the lantern on the dresser. In the daytime, with only two grimy windows, it was always dark and chilly.

From the kitchen she could hear the rasp of the pan across the stove, the shuffle of cornmeal as Nan scooped it out of the bag. She listened to the rattle of crockery and the rustling paper as Nan rooted around for some currants.

Elsie shivered, wondering if she would ever be warm again.

When she woke up, Elsie could just make out the bowl on the chair next to the bed. She pulled on her sweater and settled the bowl in the blankets between her legs. By now it was just one cold soggy lump, with a scattering of currants dotted through it like bugs.

But she ate every bit. She didn't light the lamp or go out to sit with Nan, who she could hear knitting, her chair squeaking from time to time. Instead, Elsie lay back in the bed that hadn't seemed warm since Mother had been gone.

While she had been napping, Dog Bob had crept into the bedroom. He lay in a warm lump across her feet.

The man who had stolen him wouldn't have let him go if she hadn't stood up to him. She couldn't imagine what it would have been like, coming home without her uncle's dog.

She swung her legs out of bed. Her toes curled when they touched the chilly linoleum. Nan would have called Scoop a bugger in a bag for not showing up this morning. She wanted to tell him how clever she had been to get Dog Bob back, but there'd be real trouble if Nan found out that she had been anywhere near the shantytown, especially as the Reverend Hampton, who Nan admired more than anyone else, had told her not to.

Scoop would like to know how well things had turned out, Elsie knew. But instead of getting dressed, she sat on the edge of the bed with a draft creeping across her bare legs. Refusing to stay inside where they belonged were the tears that Elsie had managed not to cry when she had been surrounded by the hoboes in the shantytown, and she'd seen Dog Bob at the end of that rope, struggling to make his way back to her. Elsie grabbed the pillow and held it against her face as she cried and cried.

She held it there until it was damp and cold with tears, and the place in her chest where they came from was all hollow and empty. She cried into the pillow until Nan's knitting needles had stopped clicking, and Elsie heard her get up from Father's creaky chair and go outside to the outhouse.

She took a deep breath and wiped her nose on the corner of the sheet. She put the pillow back on the bed with the wet side down. Then she got dressed, even though her whole body felt heavy and tired. And much older than when she'd got up from this same bed just that morning.

She pushed the curtain aside and took her bowl and spoon into the living room. She scrubbed her face with the damp washcloth and was spreading it over the edge of the washbowl when Nan came back into the house. "Feeling better, are you?" She picked up a rag from the table and chose a spoon from the pile of silverware. "Thought these might fetch a dollar or two." Nan rubbed each piece hard before returning it to the pile on the table.

Elsie leaned one hip against the table. "I thought I'd go and visit Scoop."

"One minute you're in bed asleep, being molly-coddled. Napping in the middle of a perfectly good day!" said Nan. "Now you want to go out and play?"

"I'm feeling better. Thank you for the corn mush."

"You could be helping me with this." Nan put a spoon back on the pile, then picked it up again, blew on it and gave it another brisk rub.

"Please, Nan." Elsie put one arm around her grand-mother's waist. She reached up to give her a kiss.

Nan shifted away. "That's enough of that. All right, then. Skedaddle if you must. Home by supper, mind."

Elsie shoved her hat down hard on her head and flung her jacket over her shoulder. She put one hand on the door handle and stood aside, waiting for Dog Bob to go through the door ahead of her. But instead of getting up to join her like he usually did, he just lay under the table as if he was not planning to come out anytime soon.

CHAPTER FIFTEEN

Scoop answered the door, his nose red and his hair sticking out all over the place. "Don' yell at be," he said. "I bin sick." He stepped aside so Elsie could make her way around two bicycles, a shopping basket, three boots and a baby blue sweater heaped at the foot of the stairs.

In the kitchen, Scoop's mother was sitting in the big Windsor chair with her feet up on the table—on the table!—reading a *Ladies Home Companion* magazine. "Don't expect me to get up," said Mrs. Styles. "I've been canning. You like applesauce?"

Elsie's mouth got all watery just at the sound of it.

"Two whole crates of apples last week. The father of one of our boarders grows them in the Fraser Valley." Mrs. Styles reached behind her head to retie her apron strings behind her neck. "Runty, many of them. Scabby, the others." She pushed up the nest of hair that just fell back over her ear again. "Enough for eleven jars though. One for you, if you want it."

She nodded toward Scoop, who sat huddled in a chair. "Our boy's got a nasty cold. We sent him to bed. But that didn't last."

When his mother leaned across the table to ruffle Scoop's hair, he muttered, "Gedoff," and pulled back out of her reach. "Bud I'b bedder now." He sniffed loudly.

Mrs. Styles eased herself up from her chair with the kind of sigh Nan made when she got out of bed in the morning. "I'll leave you to it. There's bread in the bin and jam in the pantry. Ernest, cold or no cold, you be a good host. Find a snack for your friend. I'm off upstairs for forty winks."

Elsie could hear thumps and laughter overhead, but she couldn't tell if it was the Noises or the lodgers. How could you sleep with all that noise?

"Nice to see you, lovie," said Mrs. Styles. She gave the brim of Elsie's hat a flick. "Come and see us again soon."

When the door had closed, Elsie poked her finger in a hole in the red-and-white-checkered tablecloth. "Where were you?" she said.

"Whadda you bean?" asked Scoop.

"We were supposed to go to the shantytown. I waited and waited. Then I had to go on my own."

"Without be?" Scoop hacked a lump of bread from a loaf with a black blistery crust. "Ma wouldn't let be out of the house. Because ob by cold." He carved a second piece of bread, then slathered them both with jam—the blackberry jam Elsie had helped make last fall with the berries they'd picked from along the railway tracks, where the shantytown was now.

"I had an adventure," she told him. "I was in a tight spot for a bit. But it all turned out well." Elsie knew she was using Nan's words; she couldn't think how else to describe what happened. She was still scared in a shaky kind of way. But proud too.

Scoop dumped the bread and jam on the table and plunked down on a chair. "Go on. Hab the biggest."

Elsie took a slab of bread and spread the glistening jam evenly right to the edge with one finger. Not all globbed in the middle the way Scoop had doled it out. She sniffed, inhaling the sweet musty smell of blackberries. If she took the time to smell the food before she ate it, it seemed to make it go further.

"So. You gonna tell be?" asked Scoop.

Elsie could just make out his question around his mouthful of bread and jam. She took a little bite of her bread, chewed each bite twenty times, and only then did she swallow it. "Me and Dog Bob went to the shantytown, and there were these hoboes. When I asked them if they knew Father, they just laughed." She took another bite of bread, chewed slowly and put her slice back on the table. "I don't know if they'd have told me if they did know him. But I don't think he was there." She pulled the crust away from what was left of her slice of bread, leaving just the soft white middle. "One of them stole Dog Bob." She rolled the bread into a lump.

"Ged away!" Scoop's eyes were big and round. They were red from his cold and very bright.

"He did! A man had him tied up to a rope. He wouldn't let go. But I made him." Elsie sat up straight in her chair and looked steadily at Scoop.

Scoop ducked his head and asked in a quiet voice, "Did you cry?" As if it would be all right if she had. But he hoped she hadn't.

"I did not." When Elsie thumped her hand on the table, the breadboard bounced a little. "I was too mad." She brought her hand down again and squished a chunk of bread. "I told them they should be ashamed of themselves. All of them. I yelled at them!" Elsie felt a giggle move along her throat, up into her mouth. It escaped in a loud shout of glee. "I told them they should be ashamed of themselves!"

Scoop laughed too, spluttering flecks of chewed bread onto the table. When his laughter turned to a cough—just like the shacker's at the shantytown—Elsie jumped up and pounded his back until he stopped.

He elbowed her aside. "I think you broke my rib," he said dramatically. Then he laughed again. "I wish I had bin there. You told 'em off. Just like your nan would hab done!"

He shoved the jam jar away, tipped his chair back and propped his knees against the table. "But you should hab waited for be to get bedder. We're a team. We could hab gone together." He took another bite, staring at the bread in his hand as he chewed.

Elsie grabbed a rag from the sink and swiped at the table. "You're disgusting. You've got bread and jam spit all over the table."

"Disgusting yourself. Eat that bread or Mother will think I was wasting food. So what habbened? Did you rescue Dog Bob?" Scoop's mouth was so red with jam, he looked like he'd been attacked by the Noises' lipstick.

"He's home safe and sound under the kitchen table. He won't come out."

"You should hab waited until I could come. I could hab interviewed those fellas. Found out bore about the life of a hobo."

"I think the Reverend Hampton is right. It feels dangerous there." said Elsie. She knew how much

Scoop hated missing out on an adventure. But she'd had one on her own, and lived to tell the tale, as Nan would say. Now she knew she could take care of herself wherever she went. But adventures were important to Scoop. Until she grew nubs like the Noises, he would be her best friend, and they needed to have adventures together. "How about we track down the story about the dance marathon?" she asked. "And this time we'll both go."

CHAPTER SIXTEEN

"I'm ready when you are, pardner," said Scoop as he cut himself another slice of bread without asking Elsie if she wanted one.

"We can't go today," Elsie told him. "Your mom won't let you, with that cold. Anyway, it's too late. And tomorrow Nan's going over to Mrs. Tipson's to change the shelf paper in her pantry. If I go and help, maybe I can earn ten cents."

"Thad'll ged you into the barathon. How 'bout I budder up the Noises and baybe they'll gibe be a dibe. Or the boarders, if I polish their shoes." Scoop's nose was streaming again. He swiped one arm across his face and sniffed loudly.

Elsie brushed the crumbs off the table and screwed the lid back on the jam jar. "Let's go on Sunday.

But I have to do my homework first," she said. "Did
you do yours?"

In Nature class, Miss Beeston had drawn a diagram
of a leaf on the blackboard, marking the ribs and veins,
the stipules and blades. At home, they were supposed
to find a leaf and diagram it the way she'd done on the
board. When Scoop said that he would rather draw
a dead body as if he could see straight through it,
Miss Beeston had told him to follow the instructions
to the letter for once.

"I haben't done by hobework. I bin sick, you know,"
he told Elsie again.

She rolled her eyes. Her leaf was pressed between the
pages of Nan's Bible.

She pushed her chair back and brushed the crumbs
from her pants. If Dog Bob were here, he'd have
cleaned up the floor after their snack. "I gotta go now,"
she told Scoop. "Do your homework so we can check
out that dance marathon. Hear?"

"Okay, pardner."

He was still sitting at the table as Elsie opened the
door to leave.

Outside the dance hall stood a billboard with *Fifth
Day* slapped across it. Elsie could hear music coming

from inside and a loud voice sounding like someone giving orders. Someone laughing. "Nan gave me a dime. Where's yours?" she asked Scoop.

His nose was still red, and he kept sniffing. Even though the sun on the street was warm, he flapped his arms up and down as if he were cold. "Don't got one."

"I thought you were going to ask your sisters. Or the lodgers."

"I was too sick to shine shoes. That's hard work. I thought you said you'd get one for helping that lady in your old house?"

Elsie hadn't told Scoop that she'd run out on Nan in the middle of the job. She couldn't bring herself to explain how humiliating it had been to crawl all over what used to be her own kitchen, to be cooped up in the pantry where she had helped her father build the shelves not so long ago. And she wasn't about to tell Scoop that Nan had said she wasn't much help and hardly deserved a dime for being so childish, then finally gave her one grudgingly only because *A promise is a promise.* Elsie hadn't dared ask for another, Nan was so aerated. Sometimes you could not tell your best friend everything. "I thought we were just coming to get the lay of the land," she said. "You said that real newspapermen do their research first."

"That's important, of course." Scoop pulled out his book and licked the end of his pencil. Then he stuck it behind his ear.

"How about I take notes this time?" Elsie suggested. "You tell me what to write."

When she reached for Scoop's book, he pulled away from her. "You're just my sidekick, remember?" he said. "*I'm* the reporter. Anyway, I don't think you'd know a red-hot story if it burned you." He stepped back to let a couple go to the door. Then he changed his mind and tapped the man's elbow. "Excuse me. Could I have a moment of your time?"

The woman took her hand from the crook of the man's arm. She patted her hair with a very pale hand with long red nails. Her blond curls were pressed tight against her head like a pretty hat, and her tiny mouth glistened with bright red lipstick.

The man ran his finger down one long black sideburn and flashed a toothy smile. "No autographs. Please."

Scoop frowned as if he didn't know what to make of this. Then, in a most un-newspapermanly way, he asked, "Who are you?"

"That's for me to know and you to find out," the man said.

The lady snickered. "I could ask the same of you, little boy."

"I'm Scoop." He puffed out his chest and drew his book from his overalls pocket. "I'm hoping to document...I mean I plan to make a record...I mean..." He sniffed and looked at Elsie, then back at the man as, all in a rush, he asked, "Can you spare a dime?"

Elsie felt herself flush red. Over and over, she'd been told that no matter how difficult things were, they would never beg. She had seen the men on the street with cardboard signs pleading for a day's work, mothers with crying children huddled around them begging for food. She knew it was because of the Depression. But she knew that begging was not the right thing for her to do.

As she grabbed Scoop's arm, the man stepped back and frowned at his companion. All Elsie wanted to do was get Scoop away from there before the man gave them his spare change. As if they were beggars. As bad as the hoboes. "Sorry to trouble you, sir," she said. "Come on, Scoop. We'll come back later."

"Hang on!" Scoop tried to pull away from her.

"No. Let's go." She struggled to keep hold of Scoop's sleeve. But he yanked back and forth, just like a dog hanging on to a rope with its teeth. She finally let go and fell back onto the sidewalk with a thump that went all the way up her back and gave her head a jolt.

When the man in the silky gray suit put out a hand to help her up, the woman said, "We're due on in ten minutes, Jake. Leave these children alone, for heaven's sake." She tottered to the door on her high heels and held it open. The man winked at Elsie, then followed the woman with a little flick of his wrist, which might have been a wave.

"Look. You ripped my coat." Scoop shoved his arm at Elsie as the door closed. "I think they were famous. They've been in the glossies, I bet. You made me miss out on a big story."

"You shouldn't have begged," she told him.

"Well, it's better than stealing," he answered, as if that idea had just occurred to him.

"You shouldn't do that either!" said Elsie.

"No one got hurt."

"*I* did." Elsie thumped him.

Instead of hitting back, Scoop stepped away from her and peered at the billboard.

"What's so interesting, anyway?" said Elsie. "It's just a dumb dance. Mother and Father used to dance. Sometimes after I went to bed I'd hear them, and I'd come down and watch. But Nan and the Reverend say what they're doing here is degrading. I don't know what that means. Do you?"

"Whatever it means, it's a story. Don't you know that?" said Scoop. "If I'm going to be a newspaperman,

I have to follow the stories. Wherever they lead." He tapped his nose and tried to wink, but only managed to scrunch up his face.

"Nan says marathons should be outlawed," Elsie said. "That it's indecent to watch people at the marathons. But she won't tell me why. How about you interview her instead? That would be research."

Scoop smacked his notebook against the wall. "Don't you get it? If they don't want us to see a bunch of people dancing, there must be a story. We can't find out about it by asking your grandmother, you dummy. What does she know! *You'll* never make a news-paperman. That's your funeral. But I've got a nose for news, and I'll be back."

He swaggered away from her, his coat flapping. "You coming or what? I'm going to find that dime one way or another, chicken!" he yelled as he marched off.

CHAPTER SEVENTEEN

It didn't take long for Elsie to catch up with Scoop. But she was so mad at him for calling her a chicken—she who had rescued Dog Bob from the hoboes!—that she ran ahead.

"Slow down, will ya?" he called. "I've been ill, ya know."

Elsie leaned against a storefront where *Out of Business* was scrawled across the window in white-wash. When Scoop finally caught up, beads of sweat sparkled across his forehead. He'd better not faint here, Elsie thought. She'd have to go halfway across town to fetch his mother. "You okay?" Maybe she'd have to find an ambulance!

He panted for a moment. "Just considering my options. Figuring out what to do." He panted some more, his hand on his chest. "I'm starving. Where's your dime?"

"Why?"

"We could get a plate of beans at Melvin's. Maybe he'll give us credit, and we can get two plates."

Elsie's stomach suddenly felt as hollow as a drum. "Maybe beans *and* a glass of milk."

Scoop was studying his jacket sleeve. "Reckon Gladdy or Belle will fix this for me before Mother sees it?"

Elsie fingered the ragged tear in the worn corduroy. "Sew it yourself. Nan'll give you needle and thread."

"Newspapermen don't sew! The only men who sew are sailors." Scoop grinned. "I'll race you for those beans. Come on."

Even though Elsie gave him a head start, she easily overtook him at the corner. By the time she reached Melvin's, Scoop was half a block behind, dragging his feet. He'd wear his boots right down to his socks, if he wasn't careful.

While she waited, Elsie peered through the café window. It was so smudgy with steam, all she could see were lumpy shapes moving around. When she put her hand on the knob, it was suddenly pulled out of her grasp, and she landed on the sidewalk. The second time today she'd ended up on her backside!

Melvin stood looking down at her. He was as big as a barrel. His grubby white apron was tied around his thick middle, and his shirtsleeves were rolled up above his thick red hands. The stained white hat on his craggy head was so crooked, Elsie wondered how he kept it on.

She pulled her own hat down tight. As she got up, Melvin pulled a cigarette from behind his ear and lit a match with one hand—a trick Elsie had seen Uncle Dannell do. He took a drag, then blew smoke rings in the air. "You got business here, missy?"

Elsie brushed herself down. "I'm waiting for my friend. We have a dime for beans." The rattle of crockery and a rumble of voices and the smell of coffee and hot grease drifted through the doorway. The bell over the door jangled as Melvin closed it on the noise and delicious smells. "Don't they feed you at home, you need to be wasting your money on my beans?"

"We can spend it if we want to." Elsie rooted in her dungarees. Then in her shirt pocket.

"Beans is fifteen cents. Look, missy. I've seen you with Dannell. He's a buddy of mine. You're welcome to dine at Melvin's, but you come with your family, hear?" He dropped his cigarette butt and rubbed it out with his boot. Then he bent down, picked up the stub and popped it behind his ear like Uncle Dannell would have done. "This your friend?"

Scoop had caught up at last. He was leaning against the lamppost, a wheezy sound coming from his chest.

"The man says we have to come with our parents," Elsie told him.

Scoop's face was streaky red, and his eyes were glittery bright.

"What's the matter with the boy?" asked Melvin.

"He's been sick. But he's better now. Aren't you?"

Scoop nodded hard without speaking.

"Well. My kitchen won't run itself," said Melvin. He put his hand on the door. "You go on home. Come back with your mother and father."

"Mother's in New Westminster," said Elsie, "and Father's disappeared."

"What's this 'disappeared'? Like some carnival trick? Poof! Just like that?" Melvin bent down and looked at Elsie's face closely. "You don't mean like that, do you?" His breath smelled of cigarettes and sausages.

Scoop had rested his bum against the window frame and was bent over, his fists on his knees. He'd got his breath back, but his voice sounded shaky. "Her mother went to New Westminster. To help an old friend on her deathbed. We thought maybe her father was at the shantytown with Reverend Hampton's hoboes. She went there—all by herself, without me—and they stole her dog, but she got him back. But her father's not there."

"Well, there's a to-do," said Melvin, scratching an itch under his hat.

"We had dandelion and potato stew last night," Elsie told him. "I had to go to Bryant Park and pick dandelions for our supper. I love beans. We don't have them at home."

"Dandelions. Things have come to that, have they?" Suddenly Melvin grinned. "Well. Lookee who's here."

The Reverend Hampton was reading his Bible as he came down the street. The same way Scoop studied his notebook until he tripped over a baby's buggy or bumped into a newspaper vendor.

She was just about to ask him whether he still had the picture of her father in his book when Scoop grabbed Elsie's arm and tried to drag her away. But she wasn't fast enough. The Reverend had seen them and was smiling as he walked toward the café.

CHAPTER EIGHTEEN

"Why, Elsie. This is a surprise," said Reverend Hampton.

"Hello, Reverend. We were just heading home."

"What about your beans, then?" asked Melvin. He had tucked his hands through the strings of the apron that ran around his middle. "These two stopped by for a bite," he told Nan's friend. "They have a dime to contribute, they tell me."

"I thought I'd look in for a cup of coffee. To warm myself up." The Reverend rubbed his hands together. "Would you children care to join me?"

Elsie couldn't think of the last time she'd been allowed coffee. Nan drank chicory these days and said there wasn't enough to go around. "We can pay. I have a dime," she told him. "We had planned to use it to get into the da…" When Scoop grabbed at her, Elsie just managed to stop herself. "We thought we had enough for beans," she said quickly.

Scoop swiped at a bead of sweat trickling down beside his ear. When he bent down to put his hands on his knees again, he nearly fell over. The Reverend caught him by the elbow. "I think this is the best place for us for the time being. It's Ernest, isn't it?"

Scoop didn't answer as the Reverend guided him into the steamy restaurant, with Elsie following. "Sweet tea. I think. And beans," he called to Melvin, who headed for the counter. "With toast for two. And one coffee."

A lady with a hat like a saggy flowerpot moved her shopping bag so the Reverend could lead Scoop and Elsie past. They found an empty table at the back, beside a young couple who were leaning so close that it looked like they might bump heads at any minute. Elsie watched them, hoping they'd kiss. But they just whispered so quietly, she couldn't hear.

Scoop was slumped back against his chair as if he was asleep. "Do you think he's all right?" Elsie asked Reverend Hampton.

The Reverend took his Bible from his pocket and set it on the table. Just as he leaned forward to look closely at her friend, Scoop's eyes popped open. "I've been ill. But I'm okay. Really." He glared at Elsie. "Don't tell my mother."

"What would I tell her?" she asked.

"Women worry. You know how it is." Was that really a wink he gave the Reverend?

Sometimes Scoop did the daftest things!

Melvin arrived with two plates piled high with beans in tomato sauce. Triangles of toast were propped up like wings at the sides, reminding Elsie of the fairy cake Mother had made her so long ago. "Did you know my mother's gone away?" she asked the Reverend. She took off her hat and set it on her knees.

The Reverend pushed a plate toward Scoop and moved the other in front of Elsie. "Your grandmother informed me. And your uncle is away working in the cranberry fields, I understand."

Scoop shoveled beans into his mouth as if he were afraid that someone might steal the plate from him. Elsie was hungry too. But she tried to eat slowly, alternating bites between mouthfuls of tea, which was very strong and very sweet. She swallowed and wiped her mouth on her sleeve. "Will you tell us about the dance marathons?" she asked the Reverend. "What's wrong with them?"

Scoop gave her a nasty look and swallowed hard, as if he was about to say something. But instead he took another bite of toast.

"It's for research," she added quickly.

"Dancing should be for celebrating. Not as a means of exploitation." Reverend Hampton put down his cup and gave his tea another stir. "These are hard times. So, of course, desperate measures are sometimes called for. But these events are aberrations. Why are you so interested in them?"

"What's aberrations? And exploitation?" asked Scoop. He squished the last bean with his fork and popped it in his mouth. He wiped his toast around the plate to get the last streaks of sauce.

When he looked across the table at Elsie's plate, she pushed it toward him. "Go on. I've had enough." She turned to the Reverend. "We want to know *about* them. What happens? Who signs up?" she said. "How can they dance for a month? That's what the sign says. Thirty days. Nan says…she says that you said that they're bad. But why? That's what we want to know."

Scoop had already finished Elsie's beans. "Have you been there?" he asked. "I mean inside, where they are dancing?"

The Reverend hauled his handkerchief from inside his coat. It unfurled like a limp gray flag. He swiped it across his face and patted his neck. "I have been to one. In Winnipeg, when they first became the fashion. I tended a few poor souls there." He frowned and shook his head. "People dance for the chance to win money. There's no pleasure in it. Just desperation."

Melvin took their cups and plates away and soon returned with their cups refilled and steaming.

The Reverend continued to talk in a low, even voice, his gaze moving from Elsie to Scoop and back again. "These dance marathons take advantage of the weak and allow the strong to exploit them. Poor people dance long past endurance for money. That is all there is to it. And people who are just as poor use their few coins to watch them. Those who do endure, who win? They are often left empty-handed. Cheated. They lose their strength and their dignity, and they end up poorer than when they started. That, children, is an aberration."

"But the poster says the winner gets a thousand dollars," said Elsie. "That's more than a car costs!" She watched Melvin polishing cutlery with his dirty apron and wondered how clean the cutlery could get. A big tea urn hissed behind the counter. A man in the corner was asleep with his face in his newspaper. Now and again the bell over the door rang as people came in or out.

"That is the lure," the Reverend Hampton said. "Greed and despair. That's what draws people to these events. A fatal combination of human frailties." He sat back, looking from Scoop to Elsie. "Would you like to go and see what I'm speaking of?" He spoke quietly, as if to himself. "Perhaps it is better to know, than to be in ignorance of the world."

"You'll take us to the dance marathon?" asked Elsie in surprise.

"First I must persuade your grandmother of the educational nature of the initiative. Let's get this boy home first, and I can speak with his parents too." Scoop was snoring, tipped in his seat as if he might fall off any minute. Reverend Hampton stood up, pushed his chair back and then picked up her friend in his arms.

"He only has his mother," Elsie told him. "Scoop's the man of the house now."

The Reverend sighed. "So many children without fathers." His gaze rested on Elsie. "Come. Let's get him home. You will need to lead the way."

CHAPTER NINETEEN

"And about time too," Nan said when Elsie came in the door. Her face was red and shiny as she stood up from the tub where she'd been bleaching sheets.

"The Reverend took us for beans at Melvin's."

"Spoiling your supper, no doubt." Nan stirred the ropy mess of laundry with her wooden tongs. "Now you're here, be of some use." She groaned as she eased her back straight and handed the tongs to Elsie. "So where is the Reverend now?"

"Taking Scoop home. He's still sick and needs to be in bed. The Reverend stopped to visit with Mrs. Styles. He'll be here shortly."

"Good. I could do with a visit myself. Today of all days."

"Why today?"

"It's no never mind to you, miss. Give that lot a good stir. Then help me truck that water out to the yard and fill the tub again. Has it stopped raining?"

Elsie nodded.

"Let's get this lot sorted out, then," said Nan. "Bring that with you." As she pointed to a bucket hanging on the wall next to a tangle of sock frames and coat hangers, an envelope dropped from her sleeve.

Elsie reached for it, but Nan got to it first. "Is that from Mother?" asked Elsie. The bucket clanked against the tub as she set it down. "Can I read it? When is she coming home? Has her friend died yet?"

"Who said she was going to die?" Nan tucked the envelope into her apron pocket and bent down to haul up a hank of wet laundry. "Don't you be getting aerated. It's not from your mother."

"Is it from Father, then?"

"Whoever it's from, it's none of your business. Mine neither. It's not addressed to me."

"It must be from one of them. Uncle Dannell wouldn't write. No one else ever sends us letters. I've been waiting so long. I need to know when Mother's coming home. I'm sick of being patient." Elsie jabbed the laundry tongs at the scummy mess in the tub, and a tear dripped down her cheek. As she stuck out her tongue to catch it, it fell with a tiny splash into the water. "I hate all these secrets!"

"Let's have no waterworks," said Nan. "And *hate*'s a strong word." She dragged a sheet from the tub, twisted it into a hank and squeezed it tight. Murky water streamed back down into the tub. "It's nothing to do with secrets," she said. "There's grown-up business. And business children need to know about. And right now there's no time for either of them." She picked up the heavy bucket. "Get that door so I can hang this lot outside."

As she and Nan fed the wet sheets through the wringer, Elsie kept peeking at Nan's damp apron and the envelope outlined against her hip. She kept her eye on it as they wrestled the laundry over the line. But she didn't mention it again. The more you nagged Nan, the more she held out. Elsie decided to wait until her grandmother took off her apron and went into the bedroom to make herself tidy for the Reverend's visit.

It took a lot of trips to get the wash hung up and the tub emptied. Elsie helped move the kitchen table and chairs back where they belonged. At last Nan shoved her arm up against her face to push her damp hair back. "I'd better make myself decent for the Reverend. You put the kettle on. And peel those spuds. There's a piece of gammon we'll fry up that will do for the three of us."

She should never have let Scoop have her left-over beans and toast, thought Elsie. She was already hungry again. Or still hungry. Sometimes she couldn't tell which. If the Reverend stayed for supper, there would be less gammon for her. Her mouth watered just thinking about its lovely salty taste.

She watched Nan pull the apron over her head and fold it across the back of the chair. She waited as Nan reached into the cupboard and pulled out a handful of potatoes and dumped them on the table. She jigged her foot as her grandmother rooted in the drawer and took out the little knife with the bone handle. "And get those eyes out too," she told Elsie. "Last time the spuds were looking at us cross-eyed all through supper."

At last Nan turned toward the bedroom. But then, with one hand on the curtain, she turned quickly, reached toward the chair and took the letter out of her apron pocket. Then she disappeared into the room beyond.

Elsie slumped into a chair. She put her feet on Dog Bob, who was dozing under the table. But even with his familiar warmth against her socks, she was still miserable with all the secrets hanging over her head like soggy laundry.

"You're all flushed," said her grandmother as she came back into the room. She rubbed her balled-up handkerchief against Elsie's cheek. "You better not be coming down with something again. Beans on your face and no potatoes peeled?" She filled the dipper with water from the tub by the door, poured water into the kettle and put it on the stove. "Get a move on, miss. You sure the Reverend planned to drop by?"

Elsie nodded and dug the knife into the potato, purposely peeling away more spud than skin. She dropped what was left of it into the pan with a splash. As she attacked another, she tried to sort out where Nan might have put that letter.

On the dresser against the wall in the old cigar box, with Nan's old photos? Most were formal studio pictures with unsmiling people standing next to tall palm trees or in front of murals of mountains. One showed her mother as a baby sitting on Nan's lap, with two serious-faced ladies standing behind. One wore a big hat so fancy it looked like a wedding cake.

But Elsie's favorite was the photograph taken at Kitsilano Beach two years ago. Father's trousers were rolled up to his lumpy knees, and his handkerchief was tied at its four corners over his head. Mother was carrying her shoes in one hand, wearing her summer frock with tiny pansies all over it. Between them stood Elsie in a knitted swimsuit that came down to her knees, with a beach bucket that Father had set upside down on her head.

She dropped her knife on the table and took her hat from the peg, jamming it down tight. She didn't care how many times Nan told her to take it off. She felt better with her hat on. She poked her finger into the pan of water and watched the potatoes bump into each other, then drift apart. She felt like that. Tiny and cold. Going round in circles trying to figure everything out.

Nan came back into the room and picked up the saucepan. "Find the cups and saucers. And set out the sugar bowl. The Reverend has a sweet tooth."

Dog Bob was at the door before Nan's friend had even knocked. He whined as he waited for the door to open, but when he saw their visitor was not Uncle Dannell, he retreated through the curtain to the bedroom.

"Did I disturb your supper?" The Reverend hung his coat up on the coatrack behind the door and wedged his hat on top of it.

"Certainly not," said Nan. "Sit, why don't you. The tea's just steeping. We were hoping you'd join us for a boiled dinner. I've a lovely piece of gammon that Mrs. Styles sent over with her boy." She brought the teapot to the table. "I hear you've been treating Elsie and Ernest at the diner."

The Reverend turned his Bible the right way about, then laid one pale hand on it. "The children and I enjoyed an interesting discussion."

"It's a rare day that boy talks sense. His late father was a printer with the newspapers. That's where that child gets his high-handed ideas, is my best guess," said Nan. "This one's got her head screwed on right. Though I worry about Ernest's influence, I do."

Elsie shifted the sugar bowl toward the Reverend, who helped himself to two spoonfuls.

The Reverend and Nan nattered about the Bradleys down the road. They were expecting another child, when they already had four and no work in the family. The food the ladies were able to cook up at the soup kitchen had got better since an anonymous donor started dropping off crates of cabbages and carrots. The church ladies were still managing to put together lovely altar arrangements. Elsie sat through their endless chat with her head resting on her arms at the table. She even dozed off for a while and only moved when Nan declared supper ready, dishing out potatoes, turnips and gammon.

There was just enough for one thin slice of meat each, with an extra one for the Reverend. "That was delicious," he told Nan as he pulled out his gray handkerchief and swabbed his face. "I thought

I might take this young lady—and her friend, if his mother gives her permission—out for the day tomorrow."

"This one has chores. And homework." Nan wiped the table and brought another pot of tea.

"Might you be able to complete your homework tonight?" the Reverend asked Elsie. "I could perhaps help."

"She doesn't need help," said Nan. Then she added quickly, "Though it's a kind offer. This one has the brains, and she needs to use them, or they will fail her when she needs them most."

"I'm almost done. And I can do my chores tonight too," said Elsie hopefully.

Nan lifted the lid off the teapot, looked inside, then set it back in its place. She looked at Elsie, then turned to the Reverend. "Well. Just this once perhaps." Then she added, "With her mother away, and her father... It's all down to me."

"And a very good job you're doing, if I may say so." The Reverend smiled at Elsie.

"And how will you spend the day with these children?" asked Nan.

"Ah. Well. In these times...I think it might be educational for the children to learn a little about how vulnerable we all are. How easily manipulated."

As he talked, humming and hawing, Elsie realized that the Reverend was scared of her grandmother!

"They should perhaps learn," he said, "of the wickedness of the world, and how it preys on the weak. So I thought...perhaps it might be a good idea...I thought I might take them along to Terminal Avenue. To the dance marathon."

CHAPTER TWENTY

Nan's cup rattled on the saucer as she put it down. "That evil place!" Her spilled tea made a puddle on the table. Elsie jumped to her feet, grabbed a rag and dabbed it up. "I can't believe this is a good idea," Nan told the Reverend.

Elsie felt all her excitement drain away like scummy water out of a laundry tub.

Nan's cheeks were mottled red. "I must say, if I may, I am surprised. You have spoken so strongly against it. In the pulpit and on the street…" Her chest heaved in and out as she got aerated. Just like Uncle Dannell and Scoop!

The Reverend held up one hand. "I recall our conversations. And I value our discussions…" Nan opened her mouth to speak, but the Reverend continued. "The children are curious. And drawn by the popular press—posters and such—that give these things a certain allure. So what I propose is this." He looked at Elsie, then back at Nan. "Tomorrow I will take the two children, Elsie and her friend Ernest—or Scoop, as I believe he prefers to be called—to learn a little about it for themselves. Under my supervision."

"It costs a quarter if you go after six o'clock," said Elsie. "I only have a dime."

The Reverend was still talking to Nan. "I will share with the children a little of how these affairs are run, and how the poor are exploited. And then they can see for themselves. How people suffer. The lengths they will go to survive." He folded his hands on the table. "Might I hope for your consent?"

"I don't know, I'm sure." Nan smoothed her apron. "I shall have to think about it. But tonight, there is another matter I hoped to discuss with you."

"Of course. You must think about it." Reverend Hampton tucked his hands deep into his sleeves and sat back in his chair. "What is on your mind?"

Nan pursed her lips. She studied Elsie across the table, and then she suddenly said, "Clear the supper things."

"But—"

"No ands, ifs or buts, miss." Nan crossed her arms. "Just get on with it."

Elsie cleared the table and put their dishes in the enamel bowl, pouring hot water from the kettle over them. Nan made more tea and brought the pot to the table as she told her visitor, "I find myself in need of your advice."

"Of course." He leaned toward her. "You have my ear."

Why would anyone want his ear? Elsie stifled a giggle.

Nan frowned at her. "Elsie. Take that dog around the block."

"Now?"

"Yes. Now."

"I just thought…"

"No more of your thoughts. It's action I want," said her grandmother. "That dog has hardly stirred all day. Off with you both while I have a word with our friend."

When Elsie slapped her leg and clicked her tongue, Dog Bob didn't budge. "Come on, Dog Bob. Let's go out." He blinked at her once, then closed his eyes.

She hauled him from under the table and dragged him toward the door. Outside, she knelt down beside him and pulled his head into her arms. "It's okay. I'll take care of you. Just like I did the other day."

At last he followed her down the path. But slowly, instead of running ahead as usual.

Elsie was headed along the street to Bryant Park
with Dog Bob at her heels when she had another
idea. Lying was bad. Stealing was bad. Being a
poor sport was bad. Eavesdropping was bad too,
Elsie knew. But what was it she'd once heard the
Reverend say? *Desperate times sometimes call for
desperate measures*?

Elsie couldn't imagine feeling much more desperate
than this.

She crept back to the garage and sidled along to the
grimy window that looked into the room where she'd
left Nan and the Reverend. She stood with her back
to the wall and listened to the hum of voices inside.
Nan and the Reverend talked for a while. She heard
a chair scraping across the floor. Then silence.

Elsie stood on tiptoes to peer through the murky
glass. The Reverend was alone at the table now, his
hands resting on his Bible. He looked up as Nan came
back into the room.

Elsie darted back so she would not be seen. The
grass here was so long, and damp from the afternoon
rain, that it tickled the skin between her boots and the
hems of her pants.

When she peeked inside again, Nan was sitting
across the table from the Reverend again. And between
them, in the middle of the table, sat the envelope.

They both looked at it as Nan spoke. Then Reverend Hampton picked it up. He studied the writing on the outside, turning it over and over before he put it down.

Elsie held her breath. She waited for someone to open it. To take out the letter and read it. But they just sat, looking at the envelope and talking in voices so low that Elsie couldn't hear a word.

She leaned her head against the wall and closed her eyes. Her legs were cold. What was in that letter? At this rate, she'd never find out.

She moved out of her hiding spot and went to fetch Dog Bob, who was snuffling under the rhododendron bushes near the Tipsons' house. While he sniffed around the mailbox and piddled against the post, Elsie studied the house. Lights were on in two rooms. In her house. What would happen if she marched up those steps, knocked on the door and asked if Jimmy knew anything about the letter? She wouldn't put it past him to have stuck his nose into anything he found in the mailbox, which both families shared.

She had been waiting forever to find out where her father was and what he had been doing since he left them. To learn if her mother was safe and sound in New Westminster. She didn't give a hoot about

Mother's friend. Daisy Newman could be dead, for all she cared. But if she had died, Mother would be home by now.

Wouldn't she?

Elsie flipped up the mailbox lid. It slapped back down. She flipped it up again. And down it came. Up *slap*. Up *slap*. Up *slap* up *slap* up *slap*.

She thought she saw a curtain twitch, so she ducked back under the dripping bushes.

Dog Bob whimpered at her feet; he wanted to get back to his safe hiding spot under the table where Nan and the Reverend were talking about the secret letter. "Hush. Just a minute," Elsie told him. "I'm thinking." She yanked her hat down so she could hardly see past the brim.

Jimmy was such a sneak, he wouldn't tell her anything. What she had to do was go home and demand that Nan tell her who the letter was from and what it said. She didn't care if it was adult business. Or if the Reverend was there and you were supposed to behave in front of company.

She was sick of secrets.

Elsie stepped out of her hiding place and tipped her head back. She didn't care who saw her. Jimmy Tipson knew what she'd do if he dared show his face.

She lifted the lid of the mailbox one last time. This time, instead of letting it drop on its own, she slammed it so hard the post shook.

She turned her back on the mailbox and the house and ran back to the garage, with Dog Bob trotting ahead. Just as she took hold of the handle of the garage door, it opened. "There you are. We have good news," said the Reverend. "I think you'll be pleased."

"What is it? What's the good news?" asked Elsie.

But before the Reverend could answer, Nan's voice came from behind him. "Is the child back? About time."

As the Reverend stepped aside to let Dog Bob pass, he smiled down at Elsie. "Your grandmother has agreed that you may visit the dance marathon."

"Just once, mind," came Nan's voice.

"Perhaps you will let your friend know that he is welcome too, if his mother will allow it. We will all go together." Reverend Hampton stood at the table with one hand on the back of a chair. "That's what we agreed, is it not?"

Nan cleared the cups and saucers from the table. "I said she can go. So she may." She dumped the tea leaves from the pot into the bucket. "Whatever arrangements you make will suit, I'm sure." She joined the Reverend at the door. "And thank you for your counsel about the other matter. You have given me a lot of think about. Now. I must get this child to bed."

It wasn't like Nan to talk so much. But as she finished tidying up their supper things and hurried Elsie to bed, she nattered on about what a good man the Reverend was, how wise his advice, how he agreed with so many of her views. How she would trust him with her life. With Elsie's too. And if he thought Elsie should see for herself what went on at the dance marathons… "It took some persuading, I must say," she told Elsie as she tucked her in. "I don't like to change my mind. A sign of weakness I can't abide. But this issue is important to him. You can go and find out what it's all about. But there's no need to be bringing stories home, you hear?"

Elsie nodded.

"And don't you worry about the price of admission. The Reverend offered. But we can't be having that. Charity, we don't need. I will provide the admission fee."

"What about Scoop?"

Nan sighed. "And for him. Even if that family is better off than we ever will be, I'll make sure he has what he needs. I don't like any of this. You be clear on that," she told Elsie. "But the Reverend has given me his advice. And I will take his opinion on this."

It wasn't until Nan had gone, and she was warm in bed with Baby in her arms, that Elsie remembered the letter.

And her plans to make Nan tell her the truth of what was in the envelope.

It had not been on the table when she came home from her walk with Dog Bob. Where had her grandmother hidden it this time?

CHAPTER TWENTY-ONE

Elsie squinted along the dark hall as Reverend Hampton led the way into Taylor's Clothing factory. They had paid at the door, coins Nan had slipped into Elsie's hands as they left the house with the reminder that, although she had given permission for this visit, she wanted to hear nothing of it when Elsie got home.

"Have you brought your notebook?" she asked Scoop.

"Course I have," he whispered. "No reporter goes anywhere without his notebook."

In the light of the lone bulb hanging overhead, Elsie could hardly read the posters that hung in tatters from the brick walls. Somewhere nearby, she could hear dripping water. She almost tripped when something scuttled past her feet.

The long, dark hallway opened up into a big room with a high ceiling. Steel beams ran along the roof. A skylight overhead was cloudy with dust and cobwebs.

Around the walls ran rows and rows of seats, starting at floor level and rising up toward the back of the cavernous room. And in the middle was the dance floor, where couples shuffled around as a gramophone crackled in the background.

The place smelled damp and stale. There was no glittering ball sending showers of light down onto the dancers. None of them wore anything like the fancy clothes or glittery jewels of the couple on the poster outside.

"This way. We must let others pass." The Reverend nudged Elsie toward the bleachers, where Scoop had already settled on a seat halfway up. His arms were clasped around his bony knees. He leaned forward, staring down at the dance floor.

Elsie had expected the pretty ballroom dancing she'd seen at the New Year's party thrown by Ruth Cohen's parents in 1929. But here there were no long leaps across the dance floor. No flying skirts of the women's gowns, dark flickering tails of the men's dinner jackets or winking shine of their black patent shoes.

She had expected a band with shiny brass instruments, the rise and dip of violin bows, a man or woman crooning into a microphone. Here, the dancers shuffled around as if they were sleepwalking, holding on to each other. They seemed to pay no attention to the gramophone playing in the background.

"The sign said they would dance for thirty days," Scoop said. "Is that why they are so tired?"

"They have been dancing for more than a week," said the Reverend in a low voice. "Their suffering is only just beginning."

"Do they dance the whole time?" asked Elsie. "Without ever stopping?"

"They are permitted ten minutes sleep each hour. And a five-minute food break every two hours," said Reverend Hampton as he arranged his black coat around him.

"What about going to the...?" Scoop started to ask.

"Where do they sleep?" asked Elsie quickly. It didn't feel right talking about bathrooms with a reverend.

"On cots backstage, I believe," he said.

Just like at home, thought Elsie, as she studied the long flowered curtain that hung behind the dance floor. It didn't come all the way down to the ground, and she could see feet moving back and forth in the darkness behind. White feet in white shoes and stockings. Nurses' legs. She remembered them from visiting Nan in hospital when she had pleurisy one winter. "Are sick people back there?" she asked.

"Those that weren't sick with hunger when they started may well be by the time they have finished." The Reverend's voice was hard and cold. He shifted on the bench. "I believe the gentleman who organized this event is very proud of the medical staff he has on hand. Though to use the word *gentleman* is very generous."

"The dancers here are luckier than some," came a voice from behind.

The young man who leaned forward between Elsie and the Reverend wore a checkered cap much like Uncle Dannell's. He was thin and blond, with a bristly mustache and very blue eyes. "You know any of them folks?" He pointed to the dance floor with a pencil, then tucked it behind his ear.

Just like Scoop! "Are you a newspaperman too?" Elsie asked.

"James Forrest. Staff reporter with the *Columbian.*"

"He's a reporter!" said Elsie.

"I heard," said Scoop. "Not the *Vancouver Sun*?"

"I see you know your papers." Mr. Forrest pushed his cap back and scratched his forehead with his pencil. "The *Columbian*'s been with us the past thirty years, and, with any luck, will edge out that other rag sooner than later."

"My friend is going to be a newspaperman," Elsie told Mr. Forrest quickly, before Scoop could start

a debate about which was the best paper. "Just like…
I forget. Who's that famous reporter, Scoop?"

"Walter Winchell."

"We're here for research," she told the reporter.
The real one.

"For an in-depth piece about this here dance marathon," said Scoop. "I have to be sure of my facts. You
know how it is."

The *Columbian* reporter shuffled across two empty
seats and shifted down one row to sit next to them.
"It's never too early to start in this business," said
Mr. Forrest. "How old are you, young man?"

The Reverend had been dividing his attention
between the dance floor below and the conversation
between Elsie and Scoop and the reporter. Now he said
to Mr. Forrest, "I brought these children here to show
them that this is not about glamour and fame. Or even
wealth."

Mr. Forrest nodded. "I couldn't agree more. But it's
a hard message to sell."

"That may well be," said Reverend Hampton. "Have
you studied the phenomenon long?"

Before Mr. Forrest could answer, Elsie said, "Scoop's
eleven. I'm eleven too. I'm older than him by three
months and seven days. Aren't I, Scoop?" But he
wasn't listening. He was leaning sideways, staring at
the notebook that lay open across Mr. Forrest's knees.

"Scoop's not a very good speller, but he knows lots of big words, and he's good at adventures," said Elsie.

"All fine qualities for a reporter," said Mr. Forrest. "And with the perfect name for a newspaperman, I must say. I see you've been taking notes."

Scoop held his book against his chest, both hands clasped across the black-and-white-marbled cover.

"But perhaps you're not ready to share your sources," the man said.

Sauces? thought Elsie. But before she could ask what he meant, she noticed that the music had changed. The song was one her mother loved. Sometimes she and Father would dance around the room while Father sang "Ain't She Sweet" into Mother's hair, making her laugh and shake her head. He knew all the words and sometimes made up extra verses to make Mother laugh even harder.

Elsie watched the dancers shuffle slowly around the floor. It seemed to make no difference to them what song was playing. One couple was hardly dancing at all, just shifting from one foot to another. When one woman broke away and crumpled to the floor, her partner pulled her back into his arms. But her feet wouldn't take her full weight; they dragged behind her and the man had to pull her along.

As the Reverend, Scoop and the reporter talked quietly next to her, the curtain behind the dance floor was pushed aside, and a man in a white coat walked toward two dancers. He put his fingers around the woman's wrist, then eased her head off her partner's shoulder and peered into her face. When he waved toward the curtain, a nurse in a crisp white uniform came forward and spoke to the woman. Her partner tried to push the nurse away, but she shook him off and led the woman behind the curtain. The man followed slowly, his shoulders slumped and his head bent.

"Why did the nurse take her away?' Elsie asked.

"The doc gets to say who's fit and who's not," Mr. Forrest answered. "That girl was likely passed out, anyway. She's not missing much."

"How could she dance if she'd fainted?"

"Her partner would have been holding her up. Somehow her legs kept going."

"Can they come back?" asked Scoop.

Why had he put his notebook away? Elsie wondered. This was all interesting stuff. He should be writing it all down.

"That couple is out of it. Eliminated. But there's lots more," said Mr. Forrest as other dancers stumbled through the curtain, some rubbing their eyes, staggering this way and that as if they were in the dark. "This lot has just had their ten minutes," said the reporter. "They do them in shifts here. Not enough cots."

"It's a disgrace," said the Reverend. "This is why I brought you children here. That poster outside and the newspaper advertisements do not reflect the truth of things."

Elsie studied the spectators gathered in groups on the bleachers or sitting alone. One man was reading a newspaper. A couple were cuddling, their faces buried in each other's collars. Two young men were laughing together, one minute watching the dancers, the next whispering and nudging each other. A woman unwrapped sandwiches and passed them to three children playing between the benches.

"Would you look at this lot," said Mr. Forrest. "But if a dime can buy them a day indoors, who am I to criticize the poor souls with nowhere else warm to go?" He stood up. "I'm glad to meet you. Especially you, young man. Scoop, isn't it?" He dug in the inside pocket of his jacket. "Here's my card." He handed one to Scoop and another to the Reverend. "I've a meeting with the organizer of this shindig. A Mr. Hayden Lyle—if you can believe that's his real name. Not that I expect to get much from him. But you, sir," he said to the Reverend, "you seem to have strong opinions. My paper would be interested in your views. May I get in touch with you? An hour of your time, at most?"

The Reverend ducked his head. "Certainly. You'll find me at St. Mary's. Leave a note if I'm not there."

The reporter skipped down and along the rows of seats, pushing past the spectators in the bleachers. When he reached the dance floor and edged around the dancing couples, they showed no sign they even knew he was there.

He disappeared behind the curtain with a quick wave.

"It seems like you've been scooped, Scoop," said the Reverend.

"Why didn't you take any notes?" asked Elsie. "You won't remember all this important stuff without notes."

Scoop kept staring down onto the dance floor, his gaze wandering from one couple to another. Suddenly he stood up and pushed in front of Elsie. His notebook was tucked tightly under his arm. "Come on. Let's go."

"We just got here," said Elsie.

"Let's go, okay?" He blocked her view of the dance floor, his face pushed toward her. "You coming, or what?"

"I think we've seen what we came to see," said the Reverend. He stood up and led the way along the row of seats, then down into the hallway.

With Scoop pulling her toward the light of the open doorway leading to the street, Elsie turned to look at the dancers one more time.

They were now shuffling around the floor to the tune of "April Showers." Another of Mother's favorite songs; she always said it was well-suited to the Vancouver weather.

But it wasn't the familiar song or the dark shadows that sent a cold chill sweeping across Elsie's shoulders. It was something she saw on the dance floor. There, shuffling around the edge with her back to the bleachers, was a woman wearing a pair of ivory dance shoes. And an orange satin shirt.

Just like the one her mother had packed in her suitcase for a visit to someone Elsie had never heard of.

CHAPTER TWENTY-TWO

"Wait up!" she called. But Scoop would not let go of her. And the Reverend was already standing in the bright doorway that led onto the street. When Elsie glanced back into the shadows, she could only see a blur of dancers drifting across the floor like ghosts.

"Just a minute!" Elsie yelled. She wanted to demand that they come back inside right this minute to check on what she had seen. She wanted to walk onto the dance floor and stand in front of the dancing couple to see if there really was another woman with the same shoes and skirt and shiny orange blouse as her mother.

But, pulled along by her friend, who would not let go, she now found herself on the sidewalk with the sound of the music fading as the door closed behind them. Scoop jabbered away, telling the Reverend how his new friend would help him get on in the newspaper world. This would be his big break. He would expose the dance marathons, make a name for himself. "They're crooked," he said. "I don't know how. But I will find out." He jigged up and down. "How about I come and meet with Mr. Forrest when you have your interview with him?" he asked the Reverend. "Don't you think that would be the best way for me to learn the trade?"

"Shut up, Scoop. Just shut up."

The Reverend and Scoop turned to stare at Elsie. "Shut up," she repeated. "Shut up. Shut up. Shut up."

"Child." The Reverend laid his hand on her shoulder.

Elsie shrugged it away. "Shut up, Scoop," she said. "I just want you to shut up." She was crying and shaking. When the Reverend tried to put his hand on her shoulder again and lead her away from a group of women who stood nearby, digging in their purses, she cried even harder. That couldn't be her mother. It must be someone who looked just like her. And if it was her mother, who was that man dancing with her? Was it her father? Had he come back without telling her?

Elsie stood on the sidewalk and cried and shook. She didn't care that Scoop was staring at her with big eyes. Or that the Reverend was looking around helplessly. "Everyone just shut up," she said again, as if there were no other words worth saying. She didn't care that the only time she had ever said them before, Nan had slapped her, leaving a red mark on her cheek that stayed there for days.

Scoop sidled up to her. "Cut it out, Elsie. Quit blubbering." His voice was shaky. "I get enough of that at home. Stop it, Elsie. Please," he said, as if he was upset too. "Look. I'll let you carry my book. I'm gonna write all kinds of notes," he said. "About what we saw. That nurse taking those people away. The dancers sleeping on each other. That there was no big lights. No fancy dancers. I'll write all about it."

Elsie's arm flew out. Anything to stop him going on and on. Her hand caught Scoop's arm, sending his notebook flying onto the ground. The pages splayed open. Loose scraps of paper scattered across the sidewalk. Among the scraps was the photograph of Elsie's father.

Elsie lunged forward and grabbed it. "That's mine!"

"Hey!" Scoop dropped to his knees on the sidewalk. But he didn't give the photo a second look. He grabbed his notebook and held it tight against his chest.

The Reverend knelt down on the sidewalk beside him. But not to pray. He groped this way and that. Picking up a scrap and handing it to Scoop. Then another. He found a small pile of them, then a single piece, adding them to the papers in his hand as he stood up. He looked at them, turned them one way, then the other. He studied them again and frowned.

When Scoop reached for them, the Reverend stared at him for a moment before he gently handed over the papers, giving them a little pat as he set them into Scoop's open hands.

Elsie was still crying. The lump in her chest was still there. But she didn't know anymore what she had seen in the dance hall. Or what she had thought she had seen. She made sure her photograph was safe in her pocket, then fished out her handkerchief to blow her nose and wipe her eyes. What should she say to the Reverend and Scoop? What if the Reverend told Nan about all the *shut ups* that had flown out of her mouth?

On the road next to the sidewalk where Scoop's notebook had fallen lay a piece of paper with squiggles all over it. She bent down and picked it up. "Is this yours?"

Scoop reached forward to grab it.

"I can't read this," said Elsie slowly as she turned it over and over, looking at both sides. "It's just squiggles. It doesn't say anything."

"It's shorthand." Scoop's face grew pinker and pinker.

"This is just scribbling," said Elsie. "It's not real writing. It's not even code."

Scoop stared at the ground and scuffed his feet. He chewed his bottom lip.

"Is it?" Elsie asked.

Standing behind him, the Reverend looked at her over Scoop's head. He closed his eyes for a second; then he shook his head as if he was trying to send her a message.

Maybe she knew what he was trying to tell her. Maybe she didn't. She just didn't care. She was so sick of secrets. "You can't write at all, can you, Scoop?" she asked. "That's why you are so lousy at spelling. Why you don't get your homework done. Why Miss Beeston gives you special work. Isn't it? You can't hardly write a word!"

The dance hall didn't matter. Even if her mother was there, dancing until she dropped for a chance to win a few dollars. Even if she could dance longer than anyone else. Right now, all Elsie could feel were the secrets that everyone was keeping from her. About her father. And her mother. About Uncle Dannell.

About the letter Nan was hiding in her apron.

And now the one about Scoop the newspaperman, who was so dumb he couldn't even write a simple sentence. He would never be a reporter. There were no important facts in his notebook.

Even her best friend was keeping secrets from her.

CHAPTER TWENTY-THREE

Elsie turned and ran.

"Just a moment," cried the Reverend.

Elsie ran harder.

"Hey, Elsie. Hold up!" yelled Scoop. She could hear him chasing her.

Elsie ran until her knees ached and her head throbbed. She ran across roads, between cars, through empty lots. She climbed over fences and raced across someone's garden, nearly knocking over a small boy playing with a toy truck.

Elsie ran past the lilac tree at the end of the driveway. Past the mailbox that was always empty, no matter how many times she looked inside. She ran under the towering rhododendrons and along the gravel path until she reached the door of the small, overcrowded place that was home.

When Elsie barged into the garage, Nan startled awake, knocking her knitting off the arm of the chair. "What's the to-do?"

Under the kitchen table, Dog Bob rolled over. He yawned, then closed his eyes again.

"Where is my mother?" yelled Elsie.

"You back already?" asked Nan.

"Do you know where Father is?"

"Will you tell me what's got you all aerated?" Nan reached down to pick up her knitting. "Stop this yelling. And take off that hat. How many times!"

Elsie's hat stayed right where it was. "What's in that letter?" she demanded.

"I was going to talk to you about that." Nan heaved herself out of the chair.

"Did you know that Scoop can't read or write?" Elsie asked her.

"I did."

Elsie felt as if all the wind had been sucked right out of her. She leaned against the table. "You did?"

"You look all done in." Nan eased Elsie into a chair. "Let's get you calmed down, shall we? Then we'll take one thing at a time."

Elsie felt like throwing up. But she'd have to get up and fetch a bowl, or go out to the outhouse. So instead, she swallowed hard and decided it was easier to stay where she was.

Nan fixed Elsie a real cup of tea, rich and dark, with three sugars. She set it on the table in front of Elsie and watched until she put her hands around the cup. "You going to tell me what's got you all upset?" Her grandmother poured tea into her own saucer and blew across it.

"You knew about Scoop?" asked Elsie.

"I've seen that book of his a time or two. Caught glimpses, anyway. Looked like double Dutch to me. You told me about them spelling tests. It adds up one way or another."

When Nan slurped her tea from the saucer, Elsie hardly cared. "But he never told me," she said. "He could have." Her breath was slower now, but her whole head felt full of hot tears.

"Course he couldn't," said Nan.

Elsie blinked at her grandmother in surprise. She felt a tear dribble down her face. "Why?"

"He looks up to you." Nan pointed a knobby finger at Elsie. "You're the smart one. The brave one. You're the survivor. Doesn't matter what happens to you, you will weather it."

"He could have told me."

"Should have, is my thinking," said Nan. "And you'd have helped him, if he'd asked for it."

"He should have asked, and I'd have helped him learn to write. And read."

"But what he should have done and what he could do were different things, see?"

Elsie didn't see. "I don't understand why Scoop couldn't tell me. Why he faked it. We're friends. Best friends. Forever, he said."

"We all have our pride," said Nan. "Your friend no less than anyone else. Now. There's something *I* need to tell *you*."

Elsie wiggled her toes into Dog Bob's fur. She had so much she wanted to tell Nan. What she'd seen at the dance marathon. What she thought she'd seen. But she couldn't be sure of anything, and she didn't know how to start. Or what to say. So now, feeling very tired, almost too tired to care, all she could say was, "What is it?"

Her grandmother reached into her apron pocket and pulled out the envelope Elsie had seen on the kitchen table. "That letter you've been nagging me about is from your father."

"Let me see." Elsie's hand whipped across the table.

Nan slapped her hand down on Elsie's before she could reach it. "It's not addressed to you, miss."

"Is it to Mother?" asked Elsie.

"It is. And it's good news."

"You said it was addressed to my mother."

When Elsie stared at her, Nan looked away. "And so it is." She adjusted the bun on the back on her head. "I explained the situation to Reverend Hampton. Explained that your mother was away, that we don't know how long she'll be gone. And with no answer to our letters…"

Now it was Elsie's turn to avoid her grandmother's gaze. The idea was getting bigger all the time, like a huge fist inside her. It *was* her mother at the dance hall. And if it really was her mother there, shuffling around the floor, Uncle Dannell was probably her dance partner. It wasn't her father at all.

Her mother and uncle hadn't been in New Westminster or Richmond. They had been right here. Just across town. But the bigger the idea got in her head, the more sure Elsie was that she could not tell anyone. Especially not Nan, who disapproved of the dances so much.

Elsie felt like she was being pulled apart. Wanting to know. Wanting to tell. Everything was so tangled up, she could not be sure about anything. If only she could climb under the table and curl up with Dog Bob. "You read the letter, didn't you?" she asked Nan.

"I did."

Elsie knew what she wanted to ask. But she couldn't. She didn't dare. If she waited, Nan would tell her.

So Elsie studied her fingers and picked at the little scab on the finger she'd nicked while peeling spuds. She ran one nail through the groove along the edge of the table. She peered underneath to look at Dog Bob, who was wide-awake, blinking up at her as if he was listening and waiting. Just like she was waiting.

CHAPTER TWENTY-FOUR

Nan was silent for what seemed a long time. Almost forever. Then at last she opened the letter and read it through to herself again while Elsie studied the writing on the envelope lying face up on the table. Her fingers tingled with wanting to reach over and pick it up. To know for sure. But instead, she waited for Nan.

"Well, then." Her grandmother's eyes were moist as she looked across the table. "I've reread this a few times these past few days," she said. "Shame is a dreadful thing." Her voice was so low, Elsie had to lean forward to hear her. "It stopped your father from coming home. Just like it stopped Ernest from telling you his secret. But you're not to blame your father. Hear?"

Elsie nodded. Even though she did not understand.

"Your father ran away. That's a cowardly thing. I won't deny that."

"Where did he go?" asked Elsie. "Does he say?"

Nan tapped the letter that now lay open between them. "Boxcar tourist he was, for a while. Jumping the trains. Traveling between cities. He fetched up in Winnipeg. Met a jeweler, an old man who had gone blind, sudden like, just before your father got to town. This man met him and gave him a place to stay. Then, when he found out your father's trade, he put him to work. Isn't that something?" Nan didn't seem to need an answer. She pushed the letter toward Elsie. "He gave your father just what he needed. Work. The pride of real work. Go on, then. You might as well read it for yourself."

But Elsie didn't need to read it now. She needed to know only one thing. She took a deep breath and asked, "Is he coming home?"

Nan got up and gathered the tea things. She set them carefully on a tray and carried it to the dresser. When she came back to the table, she said, "If your mother lets him."

"Oh." Her father would come home if her mother let him?

"But there's more," said Nan. "The old gentleman has a brother in business here. Across town, mind.

There will be work for your father there, if he wants it. So that's that." Nan groaned as she sat down. "You have to be patient just a little longer. We'll give your mother the news as soon as she gets home from New Westminster. And this too." She reached into the deep pocket of her apron. "Your father sent this to keep us going until he comes home." She held up some folded bills, then tucked them back where they'd come from.

Elsie wanted to ask how much money Father had sent. But it was rude to ask. At least it might be enough so she would not have to pick dandelions at Bryant Park again.

She chewed the inside of her cheek. Was her mother in New Westminster with Daisy Newman? Or was she at the dance marathon? She had to find out so she could tell her about the money. And the letter from Father.

Surely, she would let him come home.

"You look like you've perked up," said Nan.

"I feel a bit better."

"What do you plan to do about your friend? He's a handful, that's for sure. But a person can't help but be fond of the boy. Be sad if that friendship went out the window." Nan opened the door for Dog Bob and watched him trot outside. "That dog's back to his old self, looks like. And you, miss. Take that hat off. How many times." She picked up her knitting.

Elsie twisted her hat between her hands as she sat in Father's chair and thought about secrets. She had to keep hers to herself, for now. Until she was sure. But she needed to talk to Scoop about his secret. At least check that he was still talking to her after the argy-bargy outside the dance hall.

Maybe he couldn't read. Or write. But she could. Maybe he'd never be a newspaperman.

But she was his friend. Friends helped each other. And she was bright. Nan said so. She would help Scoop learn to read and write.

But first she had to go back to the dance marathon, to be sure about what she had seen. And Scoop would want to be there when she found out the truth about who was shuffling around the floor at Taylor's. If her mother was there, she could tell her about Father. And the money. That would make her come home. And with Father home too, the family fractions could work out at last.

"How much did Father send?" Elsie asked her grandmother.

"Household finances are none of your business, young lady."

"What did you get for the silverware, then?" Elsie picked at a loose thread on the arm of the chair.

"A dollar or two," said Nan.

"Thank you for the money for the dance hall," said Elsie.

"Mmm. A pleasure, I'm sure. You didn't tell me how you got on."

"It was interesting," Elsie told her. Nan seemed to have forgotten that she wanted to know nothing about it.

"That all?"

"We met a reporter. A real one from the *Columbian*. He's going to interview the Reverend for a story about dance marathons."

"That would be the story your friend was after, eh? Beaten at his own game. That will be a blow for the young man."

Maybe that's why Scoop had been so quiet in the dance hall, thought Elsie. And outside. She remembered his face as his book and notes scattered all over the sidewalk. It gave her a sad twinge to think of him without his big plans and schemes, especially now that people knew that his notes were all just nonsense.

"I hadn't thought of it like that," said Elsie. She got up and moved to sit on the arm of Nan's chair, leaning against her warm shoulder. "Can I have a dime, please?"

Nan shifted her elbow as she turned her knitting. "What for?"

"I have to go back to the dance hall. Just this last time." She waited for Nan to say something, but her needles were clicking away as fast as ever. "I want to help Scoop get his story. I want him to scoop the other reporter.

He can dictate, and I'll write the story. Just like Miss Beeston does in class. Can I? Can you spare a dime?"

Nan studied the mud-colored sweater she was knitting. "You'd need two, I expect."

"Yes, please. Oh, thank you, Nan."

"I'm doing this for the boy." Nan prodded Elsie gently with her knitting needle. "I can only imagine how he feels, shown up in front of his best friend. Be gentle with him, mind." She put her knitting in her lap and looked at Elsie. "What are you waiting for, miss? I could be doing with you out of my hair while I get this floor cleaned."

The floor looked just fine to Elsie.

"And take that nasty thing with you," Nan said, pointing to Elsie's hat sitting in the middle of the table.

CHAPTER TWENTY-FIVE

A flurry of Noises pushed past Elsie as she walked up Scoop's front path. The girls giggled and called out to each other in their high fluty voices. One of them—Elsie thought it was Lilly, but she could never be sure—said, "Hi, Elspeth," to her as she danced down the street. They should know her name by now! There were so many of them, but only one of her.

Mrs. Styles nodded toward the stairs as she let Elsie in. "He's upstairs. I think he's under the weather again. You can go on up this once."

Elsie could tell which was Scoop's room by the picture of an airplane on his door. Inside, she had to duck to avoid the paper planes hanging from the ceiling. "How many are there?" she asked.

"Thirty-seven. You should have knocked." Scoop was lying on his back on his unmade bed, with his arms under his head. "What do you want?"

The only chair in the room was heaped with clothes and towels. An empty plate teetered on top. "Budge over so I can sit down," said Elsie.

Scoop moved an inch. No more. "What do you want?" he repeated. Instead of looking at her, he stared up at the ceiling.

Before she could think of the best way to say it, Elsie blurted out, "It doesn't matter if you can't write or read. I don't care." When Scoop rolled over and turned his back on her, she said, "But you could have told me. You should have."

Scoop muttered something.

"What?"

"I said I don't care what matters to you."

Each plane hanging from the ceiling was made out of newspaper. On some, Elsie could see small advertisements. On others, parts of headlines. "I can help," she said.

Scoop turned back toward her. "Help how?"

"I can help you learn to read and write," she told him.

"It's hopeless. I'm dumb. Anyway. Who cares about dumb old writing. I'll never be a reporter. I bet I couldn't even be a printer like my dad."

Elsie studied the dangling airplanes. "What did you think of the dance marathon place?" she asked.

Scoop sat up and wrapped his arms around his knees. "It gave me the creeps, if you want to know. Maybe because of what we saw." He still wouldn't look at her. "Maybe because of what your Reverend said. Or that other man. The reporter from the *Columbian*." He sneered. "That rag."

"How about this, then?" said Elsie, ignoring Scoop's grumpy voice. "How about we go back? To check it out properly. Ask all the questions you want. We can interview the Reverend too. Just like that Mr. Forrest. Then you dictate the story to me. And I'll write it.

"That's not real writing."

"Sure it is," said Elsie. Although she wasn't sure at all.

"I tell the story, and you write it down?" asked Scoop. "What about the interviews? Someone has to write down what people say."

"I can do that too."

"Then it will be your story. Not mine." He slumped facedown in his blankets.

Elsie poked his back. "I'll be your assistant. Your sidekick, like Uncle Dannell said."

Scoop turned over and looked up at her. "Why?"

"Why what?"

"Something's going on." At least he was looking at her now. "Why would you want to be the assistant when you could do the whole job yourself? Be a lady reporter. I bet you want to be the first one ever on the *Vancouver Sun*."

"You are so dumb." As soon as Elsie said it, she wished she'd bitten off her tongue. "I don't mean that. You're smarter than smart. But maybe I want to help you."

"But why?"

"Because I'm your friend. And because…"

"What's wrong with you?" asked Scoop. "Cat got your tongue?"

Could she tell him? Elsie looked down at her hands. He was her friend. She was his best friend until she grew nubs. She should be able to tell him anything.

Scoop swung his legs over the side of his bed. "You gonna tell me or not?" He looked around the room. "Seen my shoes?" Elsie bent down and peered into the dark under his bed. She pulled out one boot, then the other, and handed them to him. "You can't tell anyone else. Not yet. Specially not Nan."

"So tell me."

"You have to promise."

"All right." Scoop held out his little finger. She linked hers around it. They shook.

"I think Mother is one of the dancers," Elsie said.

Scoop got busy shoving on his boots, tying up the laces. "I know," he said quietly. Almost to himself.

"What?"

"I said, I know. Least, I think I saw her."

"Me too!" said Elsie. "Just as we were leaving. Why didn't you say?"

"I didn't know what to say. That's why I wanted to get out of there in a hurry."

"How about the Reverend?" asked Elsie. "You think he saw her too?"

"He'd have said, wouldn't he?"

"I guess so. Well. I have to find out if it's really Mother dancing in that marathon. And if it is, you have to help me get her out of there. I saw her shoes. And her blouse. And you know what else?"

"What?" Scoop got off the bed and hiked up his pants.

"I think the man dancing with her is Dannell."

"Course it is!"

"I thought he was picking cranberries," said Elsie.

"You were conned, you were. And your nan. Hey. That's some story," said Scoop. The old Scoop. All shiny eyes and big ideas. "Maybe it will make the front page. Can you see the headline? *Mother Abandons Daughter to Dance!*"

"We couldn't. Nan must never know," said Elsie.

"Okay, then. We'll keep her name out of it." Scoop paced around the room. He flicked each little plane overhead as he passed, until they were all swinging. "Your mother went away," he said. "But she never went to New Westminster. That's why she never wrote to say she got there."

"I know that. And Uncle Dannell had a newspaper!" Elsie remembered it in a flash. "He cut out something. One minute he was all down in the dumps because he lost that money and Nan said he had to go. Then he said he was going away to work."

"He'd found out about the dance marathon. I bet that was it," said Scoop. "Now. We need to pin down this story. Put it to bed. And you know what?" he asked Elsie.

"What?"

"When the story is published, we'll put both our names on the byline."

"The what?"

"Don't you know anything? It's who it's written by." Scoop scrawled across the air, as if he was writing more gibberish. "By cub reporters Scoop Styles and Elsie Miller. Or Elsie Miller and Scoop Styles." He looked at Elsie. "No. It sounds better the other way. What do you think?"

"You can have your name first. I don't mind." After all, being a newspaperman had been his idea.

"I knew you'd see it that way. Now, let's make plans."
Scoop frowned at her. "One problem. We need twenty
cents to get in again. How are we going to get that?"

"Nan sold some silverware." Elsie showed him the
two dimes.

"We're in business!" said Scoop. As if it was all his idea.

CHAPTER TWENTY-SIX

By the time they got back to the dance marathon, it was after six, but they persuaded the fat man at the door to let them in for a dime each.

All the way there, Elsie and Scoop had debated whether to sit right at the front, where they could see the dancers' faces, or at the very back, where there was no chance of being seen by Elsie's mother and uncle until they were ready to be seen. Elsie won the argument by saying that she had the money, so she chose to sit right up at the back, way up high, where it was darkest. From there, they had a view of the whole dance floor.

By now, the bleachers were crowded. The noise of the spectators almost drowned out the scratchy music the dancers were ignoring. Near Elsie and Scoop sat a woman with two children, one sleeping against her side, the other leaning forward to watch the dancers. One man had his dog with him, lying right next to him on the bench. If Dog Bob had come along, he would have sniffed out Uncle Dannell in a minute. But Elsie had good instincts too.

"Stop fidgeting," she told Scoop.

"I'm looking for that reporter."

"Can you see who's dancing?"

"They all look the same from up here," Scoop answered. "That's hardly dancing. It's even slower now."

"They must be dead tired," said Elsie. "It seems cruel, it does, making them dance all day." She watched a handkerchief fall from a dancer's sleeve and drift onto the floor. No one picked it up. When a woman's heel tipped, her shoe fell off, but she kept dancing. One man was being held up by his very fat partner, his face almost completely buried in the lady's large chest.

"I don't think they're here," said Elsie as she studied each couple on the dance floor. "We must have imagined it."

"I know what I saw," said Scoop. "Some might be out back sleeping in shifts, like the Reverend said."

"You think so? Maybe that's where Mother and Uncle Dannell are," said Elsie. "We'll wait until they come back out."

Just then the music stopped, and all Elsie could hear now was the shuffling of feet around the dance floor, and the audience's chatter. The dancers hadn't even noticed that the music was no longer playing.

"Look!" Scoop's sharp elbow nudged her arm.

Elsie had also seen the fancy couple come through the curtain.

"It's those toffs we saw that day," said Scoop.

"I know. Sshh."

The couple moved toward the front of the dance floor. "Ladies and gentleman," the man announced. He waited until most of the chattering and laughing from the audience died down. "As you will see, the number of dancers is dwindling. The wheat has been separated from the chaff. The weak from the strong. Only the strong and the valiant remain."

Elsie couldn't see anyone who looked strong. And she had no idea what *valiant* meant.

The man went on. "As this event moves inexorably toward its conclusion, my partner Letty Driver and I would like to perform for you."

Inexorably? Even if he couldn't write, Scoop would know what it meant. She'd ask him later.

The dancers were hardly moving now. They just rocked in place, their heads resting against each other's shoulders and chests. As if none of them had noticed that the fancy couple had upstaged them.

"Let's give our friends here a short break. And a show of our appreciation." The man clapped, his partner's hand dropping from his elbow as she joined in. The audience—those who were listening and watching, and not too busy gossiping or eating—clapped too.

The fancy couple stood aside as two nurses came through the curtain, moved across the dance floor and led the dancers away. As if they were children, thought Elsie. Or dogs.

Then the man took Letty Driver's hand and turned her in a big circle until she was standing next to him in the center of the dance floor. As he drew her into his arms, she rested one hand on his shoulder and placed her other in his outstretched hand. She turned one way and stretched out her foot a little way ahead. The man did the same.

The chattering of the audience subsided.

"They look like statues," whispered Elsie.

"They're waiting for the music," said Scoop.

Someone in the row ahead giggled as the silence continued. Then suddenly the gramophone started again. First a hissing crackle. Then a familiar tune. "I know that song," said Elsie.

"They're not very good, are they?" said Scoop. He was right. One minute the woman was trying to keep up with the man. And in the next moment, his steps lagged behind hers. No bright glittering ball sent showers of light down onto them, as it had on the poster. And although Elsie caught a glimpse of a ring flashing on the man's hand, these dancers looked almost as dowdy as the other couples.

At last their turn was over. They bowed to the audience, although not many people paid much attention. The woman stood with her hand tucked into the man's arm as they watched more dancers shuffle through the curtain onto the dance floor.

"I don't know what all the fuss is about," said Scoop. "Those toffs were no better than the others. You wanna go now? They're not here, you know. I've looked and looked. We must have imagined it. Anyway. I'm hungry."

"Mother must be here. She must."

"I don't see her."

"Just wait, will you!" Elsie felt like a lump of cold clay as she stared at the sad bunch of dancers who seemed to hardly know they were being watched. Or if they did, didn't care. The thought that she had been mistaken, that Uncle Dannell and Mother were not here, that no one knew where they were, made her whole body so heavy she could hardly get up.

"What's this, then?" said Scoop.

The fancy man stood in front of the dancers, looking up into the audience again. "We now have a special treat. This is the time when you, the audience, have the chance to see the very special talent of our competitors here," he said. "Now's your chance to send down pennies from heaven." He looked up into the high rafters and laughed at his own little joke. "My friend here will randomly select one lucky couple who will perform their party piece. Just as Miss Driver and I did for your entertainment and amusement."

"I wasn't very entertained." Scoop's voice was so loud that two women turned around and frowned at him. A man farther along their bench laughed.

"Hush," said Elsie. "I want to see what's going to happen."

The man was still speaking. "We ask that you shower our talented competitors with whatever few coins you can spare. Silver Rain, we call it. So, as you can imagine, to make the best show today, nickels and dimes are most welcome."

"Have you got any more money?" asked Scoop.

Elsie ignored him.

"Let's acknowledge the talent we have here before us," said the man. "Our fortunate pair will be permitted to keep your contributions, so I'm sure you will be generous." He turned to his partner. "Miss Driver. Who is to be today's lucky couple?"

She stepped across the floor and circled the dancers. Then she stopped beside one pair and put her arms around them.

For a moment, the man staggered as if he might fall. But when his partner touched his arm, he stood a little straighter.

Elsie gasped. He was thinner than she remembered. But she recognized the man's sandy hair and the thin mustache above his top lip. Uncle Dannell!

"Ouch. Leggo!" Scoop peeled her fingers from his knee, and Elsie clenched her hands in her lap. She held her breath. If that was Uncle Dannell, surely his partner must be…

The woman at Uncle Dannell's side lifted her head as if it was too heavy for her neck. She set her shoulders back and took a deep breath that seemed to draw air right from the bottom of her feet. Elsie watched, hardly daring to breathe as Uncle Dannell stood closer to the woman as she began to sing, her voice so thin and wavery that if Elsie had not already known the song by heart, she might not have recognized it.

Her mother was singing a song she and Father often danced to. "Ten Cents a Dance," it was called. Which was just what she and Scoop had each paid to come in!

"I knew it!" whispered Scoop. "There's your mother."

Elsie couldn't answer. She couldn't even move. All she could do was watch the singer take another deep breath to start another verse.

"Mother!"

Only when Scoop hissed, "And that's your uncle too!" did Elsie realize she had spoken aloud.

She stood up and called, "Mother!" Her cry echoed into the rafters above her head, loud enough for the people around her to turn toward her. And for the singer below to stop, as if she had woken from a long sleep, to look around the bleachers that surrounded the dance floor. And then to gaze up. Up, up. To where Elsie stood.

"Mother!" Elsie waved to her mother, who seemed so far away.

The sudden noise that followed was like the buzz of a thousand bees. It was, in fact, the sound of dozens of voices telling Elsie to sit down, to be quiet, so they could hear the rest of the song. And of others calling for quiet so the dancer could hear her daughter's voice.

Elsie turned this way and that as the noise of the crowd rose toward the ceiling. Then, in a lull, she heard her mother's frail voice calling up to her, "Elsie?"

"It's me, Mother. It's me…"

Through the titters and chatter, Scoop yelled, "Be quiet. Everyone. Hush. Let her finish her song!" His bony hand gripped Elsie's, crunching the bones in her fingers together. "Let her finish. So people can throw down the Silver Rain. Pennies from heaven, just like the man said." He yanked on Elsie's arm, urging her to sit down.

She yanked back until he let go. She stared down through the shadows to the dance floor below, where her mother stood with Uncle Dannell beside her.

Scoop's fingers found Elsie's again and gave them another hard squeeze. "Let her finish," he hissed.

Elsie looked around at everyone who had turned to stare at her. She looked back down toward the dance floor below. Now that she had found her mother and Uncle Dannell, she could wait a little longer. "All right. Sing, Mother," said Elsie. She cleared her throat and called again more loudly, her voice ringing out like a bell to where her mother and uncle stood at the edge of the dance floor so far away. Her words sailed through the air, as clear as day. "Finish the song, Mother."

Then Elsie took off her hat and sat down with it held tight in her lap. Scoop sat beside her, holding her hand as her mother's lovely voice, getting stronger and stronger as the song went on, drifted toward her, as if she was singing for Elsie alone.

When she was done, Mother stood with Uncle Dannell's arm around her, looking up at Elsie. Elsie and Scoop clapped and clapped, their applause drowned out by the cheers and applause of spectators standing in the bleachers all around them.

As the applause died, one coin fell through the air. It landed on the hard ground like a drop of rain on a roof. Then another coin and another fell in a shower, spinning and turning, glinting and shining. Until Elsie's mother and uncle stood in the downpour of coins that flew through the air and fell at their feet, rolling across the floor until all around them the Silver Rain lay like bright puddles after a storm.

CHAPTER TWENTY-SEVEN

Elsie scurried over the rows of seats, pushing between chattering spectators to make her way down to the dance floor. She rushed to her mother and put her arms around her and held her tight, while her uncle rested his hand on her back, not saying a word. Scoop scuttled across the floor on his hands and knees, scrambling for every dime and nickel that had been thrown down.

The fancy man tried to persuade them to go back to their seats so the dance could go on. Letty Driver's bright mouth gleamed as she bullied Mother and Uncle Dannell with all kinds of fancy words like "breach of contract" and "reneging on agreements." Finally, a man in a shabby tweed coat barged out from behind the curtain and threatened to have Scoop and Elsie arrested for trespassing. "Get out of here, you brats!" he shouted. He gave Elsie a hard shove in the back. "You're interfering with the proceedings."

"You should be ashamed of yourself!" Elsie screamed at him. She was not surprised by the words that flew out of her mouth. And Scoop didn't even look up from the floor. But Mother and Uncle Dannell stared at Elsie in surprise.

"Can't you see you almost killed them?" she shouted at the dance marathon man. "This isn't dancing. It's true what the Reverend said. This is just explode…it's explo…"

Scoop stood up, his pockets jingling. "Exploitation," he said. "That's what it is. You've been taking advantage of everyone. This is a crooked deal. Anyone can see."

A call from the bleachers of "Hear, hear!" was followed by a loud mixture of hoots, cheers and applause.

"Exploitation. That's the word," said Elsie. "It's exploitation. Now I'm taking my mother and uncle home. And you can't stop me."

At first Uncle Dannell tried to argue. "We're almost there, I can feel it," he said. Just like he talked about all the other schemes that got him in trouble before.

Ignoring him, Elsie took Mother aside. "Nan has some news," she said. "There's a letter from Father."

Her mother's tired face brightened as Elsie went on to whisper about the dollar bills tucked in Nan's pocket.

"Let me tell your uncle," said Mother when Elsie had finished. She put her thin hand on Uncle Dannell's arm and talked quietly into his ear. So quietly that no one else could overhear. But it was not as if Mother was telling Elsie's uncle a secret, thought Elsie. This was family business.

Uncle Dannell finally nodded and patted Mother's arm. He hugged Elsie without saying a word and nodded once at Scoop, who had just pocketed the last dime from the floor. Then Uncle Dannell walked through the curtain and collected Mother's and his belongings.

Elsie, Uncle Dannell, Mother and Scoop left the dance hall together while Mr. Hayden Lyle sputtered and swore, and, all around them, the crowd chattered like a flock of startled birds.

"Elsie looked for you everywhere," Scoop told her mother and uncle when they were out of sight of Taylor's Clothing factory. It took them a while, as Mother and Uncle Dannell walked so slowly.

Scoop was being the gentleman and was carrying their bags.

"I looked for Father too," Elsie said. "I went to the shantytown. But he wasn't there." Elsie rubbed her thumb across Mother's palm. "Then we found out about the marathon, and the Reverend took us to see it, and I thought I saw you. That's why we came back. Then Nan got a letter. She wouldn't tell me who it was from at first. She said it was grown-up business." She was getting everything mixed-up. But there was so much to tell. "And I'm not like Dog Bob. I don't have the instincts to keep everyone together. But I tried. The letter came ages ago, but Nan didn't tell me about it until today. It was a secret," she added.

They stood in a huddle on the sidewalk while Mother and Uncle Dannell took a breather. Scoop sat on Mother's suitcase. Uncle Dannell picked up a cigarette butt from the pavement and flicked the dust off it, just like Elsie had seen hoboes do a million times. Mother's fingers were tight on Elsie's shoulders now. "You told me about the letter from Father. And about the money. But is he coming home?" She leaned over to stare into Elsie's eyes. "If you know, you must tell me," she said. "Even if she told you not to say, I will make it right with Nan."

At her mother's words, it felt as if all the weight she had been carrying around since Father left and Mother and Uncle Dannell disappeared and Dog Bob got stolen was suddenly lifted off Elsie's shoulders.

Like a huge sack she no longer had to carry. She felt so light she could fly away. "The man Father works for in Winnipeg has a brother in Kerrisdale. He'll give Father a job. So he can come home. If you let him, he will come home."

Elsie held her breath as her mother turned her wedding band on her finger and frowned into the distance.

Scoop was watching them now. So was Uncle Dannell.

"Can Father come home?" Elsie asked. She felt as shaky as she had standing in front of the hoboes in the shantytown. "Can he?"

Her mother turned slowly toward Elsie and touched her shoulder, her face still serious. Elsie didn't dare move as she felt her mother's fingers stroking her cheek.

At last Mother smiled—so widely it was if her whole face changed. Once again she looked like the person Elsie had known before the Depression came. Before the bank took away the jewelry business and the Tipsons bought their house. Before they moved into the garage and Father ran away.

"Of course he can," said Mother quietly. "Isn't it what we wanted all along?" She bent down to pick up her suitcase, but Scoop beat her to it. "Now, don't you think we should hurry?" she said.

"Your grandmother will be wondering where you are. We all have a lot to tell her."

We'll tell Nan everything, thought Elsie. Whether she likes it or not.

Finally the family fractions will work out. And there will be no more secrets.

"There's a dog waiting for me, I hope." Uncle Dannell waggled his eyebrows at Elsie. "I'm sure you've been taking care of him the way you promised."

When Scoop opened his mouth to speak, Elsie quickly grabbed her mother's suitcase from him. "I'll carry this." The story of how she saved Dog Bob from the hoboes could wait for another time.

Mother looped one arm through Uncle Dannell's arm. "Come on. We're dead on our feet."

"Hey, Scoop. Where's all the money you picked up?" asked Elsie, as she hauled the suitcase along.

Scoop put down Uncle Dannell's duffel bag and shoved his hands in his pants pockets. They jingled as he shook them. "It's all here. Every penny and nickel and dime of the Silver Rain."

"Let's hope there's enough to pay your nan that nine dollars I owe her," said Uncle Dannell.

For a moment Elsie couldn't think what her uncle meant. Then she remembered the argy-bargy with the pay-packet raffle. "Nan will have to let you come home too, won't she?"

They were at their own driveway now. This time Elsie did not even glance at her old house as they passed it. She couldn't care less if Jimmy Tipson was staring down at her from the bedroom that used to be hers. She didn't need to check the mailbox.

She set Mother's suitcase on the ground and pulled her hat down tightly on her head. Then, picking up the luggage and looking straight ahead, Elsie led her family home.

DANCE MARATHON CLOSED DOWN

LOCAL CHILDREN EXPOSE RACKET THAT INFLICTS INDIGNITY AND DEGRADATION

BY JAMES FORREST WITH FILES FROM "SCOOP" STYLES AND ELSIE MILLER
SPECIAL TO THE COLUMBIAN

VANCOUVER, MARCH 16, 1932. With great daring and enterprise, two local children, Elsie Miller and Ernest (Scoop) Styles, both 11, recently gained access to the dance marathon taking place in the old Taylor's Clothing building on Terminal Avenue. There, they learned more than any child should know about what desperate people are willing to do to make money to feed themselves and their families.

"Dancing should be for celebrating. Not as a means of exploitation," says social activist Reverend Hampton of St. Mary's church, Oak Street. "In these places, people dance beyond endurance for the chance to win what is advertised to be a significant prize."

But as the children found out, that money is rarely available to the dance 'winners.' Huge sums are deducted for the dancers' food, nursing care, even the cost of renting a cot for ten-minute breaks every hour during the marathon dance. Many marathons last as long as 30 days.

continued on page 16

continued from page 3

"I might not approve of how they went about it," says Nan Davies, 69. "But my granddaughter and her friend showed great tenacity when they set out to find out where my daughter had gone, when she signed on for the marathon as a way out of our present position."

Thanks to the intervention of these two young people, Mrs. Davies's daughter, Peg Miller, is now happily returned to home and hearth, enjoying a heartwarming reunion with her family. And the household situation is likely to improve with the return of Mr. Miller, who in the past months found employment in Winnipeg in his chosen profession. He returns home, and to an offer of employment in Vancouver, on Thursday.

Fraud charges are pending against the marathon organizer, Mr. Hayden Lyle of London, Ontario.

ACKNOWLEDGMENTS

Barry Broadfoot's *Ten Lost Years 1929-1939: Memories of Canadians Who Survived the Depression* provided me with insights into what life was like for so many people in the Depression, told in their own voices.

As always, I must thank Douglas Brunt for his patience and encouragement, and my editor, Sarah Harvey, who helps bring out the best in my writing and the stories I want to tell.

LOIS PETERSON wrote short stories and arti-
cles for adults for twenty years before writing *Meeting
Miss 405*, her first novel for children. Her next children's book was *The Ballad of Knuckles McGraw*. She
was born in England and has lived in Iraq, France
and the United States. She now lives in Surrey, British
Columbia, where she works as a fundraiser and in
a public library, writes, reads and teaches creative
writing to adults, teens and children.